"He'll have to go through me to get to you, Kayla."

"Thank you, but I don't want anyone to get to anybody," she countered.

"One way or another, this will come to a head," he warned her.

"Yes, it will."

He turned and eyed her warily. "You sound as if you're hoping it does."

"I am," she answered honestly. "I want him caught and questioned. I want to know why he shot me. I need to know if he had anything to do with Ty and Trey's deaths." She held his stormy gray gaze. "I hope to one day get back to living my life, whatever that means."

"I know you want answers—"

"No, I'll have answers. I told you before and I'll tell you again—I won't hide forever. You need to come up with a plan to flush the killer out of the underbrush, or I will."

"Sounds like a threat," he growled.

"No, Ryan, it's not a threat," she said without the slightest hint of rancor. "It's a promise."

OZARKS WITNESS PROTECTION

MAGGIE WELLS

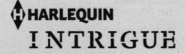

HARLEQUIN

INTRIGUE

For Julie. You are everything light, bright and beautiful, and I am thrilled to call you my friend. Team Awesome rules!

HARLEQUIN®
INTRIGUE™

Recycling programs for this product may not exist in your area.

ISBN-13: 978-1-335-58274-4

Ozarks Witness Protection

Copyright © 2023 by Margaret Ethridge

For questions and comments about the quality of this book, please contact us at CustomerService@Harlequin.com.

Harlequin Enterprises ULC
22 Adelaide St. West, 41st Floor
Toronto, Ontario M5H 4E3, Canada
www.Harlequin.com

Printed in U.S.A.

By day, **Maggie Wells** is buried in spreadsheets. At night, she pens tales of intrigue and people tangling up the sheets. She has a weakness for hot heroes and happy endings. She is the product of a charming rogue and a shameless flirt, and you only have to scratch the surface of this mild-mannered married lady to find a naughty streak a mile wide.

Books by Maggie Wells

Harlequin Intrigue

Arkansas Special Agents

Ozarks Missing Person
Ozarks Double Homicide
Ozarks Witness Protection

A Raising the Bar Brief

An Absence of Motive
For the Defense
Trial in the Backwoods

Foothills Field Search

Visit the Author Profile page at Harlequin.com.

CAST OF CHARACTERS

Kayla Powers—The second wife of Tyrone Powers Jr. A former attorney at Powers, Powers & Walton. Now the prime target of her husband and his nephew's murderer.

Ryan Hastings—Sergeant at the Arkansas State Police Protective Services Division. He is tasked with keeping the headstrong widow alive until they can capture a killer.

Delray (Del) Powers—The Senator's son. Generally believed to be the next in line to control the Powers family business ventures. He's also the man Kayla believes tried to shoot her.

Senator William Powers—Younger brother and uncle to the victims. His campaign fundraising group is the target of an FBI investigation led by Special Agent Michelle Fraser into campaign finance violations.

Michelle Fraser—An undercover FBI agent investigating financial crimes laundered through Powers, Powers & Walton. She is Kayla Powers's attorney and best friend, running her investigation while staying at the helm at the firm while Kayla is in hiding.

Ethan Scott—Lieutenant at the Arkansas State Police Criminal Investigation Division. Ethan is the lead investigator into the double homicide involving Tyrone and Trey Powers.

Chapter One

Kayla Powers never imagined there would be a day when she'd consider a half-mile walk down her driveway to be meditative, but then again, her life was full of surprises these days. Some good, some horrifically bad. Some simply…surprising. She pressed her hand to her stomach and drew in a deep breath of fresh air.

Sobriety made a person look at things in a different light.

Before now, she would have never labeled herself an alcoholic. She'd been a rebellious drinker in high school, a party girl in her undergrad days and an I-earned-this tippler all through law school. After she'd entered the workforce, she'd slid effortlessly into the postwork-drinks crowd, and later into the wives-gathered-in-the-kitchen-swilling-wine set. But until she'd watched the footage captured by the security cameras the weekend her husband and his son were murdered, she'd never considered her drinking an issue.

Talk about a wake-up call. And only the first of many.

She bent to pick up a particularly vivid leaf from a red maple and twirled it by its stem. Nearly two months had come and gone. Time was flying and moving at a snail's pace all at once. Due to the nature of Tyrone's murder and the subsequent ongoing investigation, she hadn't been able to submerge herself in the details of death—the suitable black dress, the music selections for the memorial service, what food they'd provide for her fellow mourners. Looking back on it now, it felt like she'd gone from the discovery of their bodies into the deep end of the ocean.

Only the presence of her right-hand woman and newly minted best friend, Michelle Fraser, kept her grounded. But the thought that woke her early in the morning wasn't one she'd dared speak aloud. Not even to Michelle, who was not only her friend, but also Kayla's personal attorney and therefore bound by attorney-client privilege to keep her secrets. She couldn't. Not until she was certain.

Michelle was an undercover federal agent and attorney who'd embedded herself in the fabric of Powers, Powers & Walton. Even after her investigation had revealed the financial crime of the law firm's elder statesman, Harold Dennis, and cast dark shadows over the Powers name, she'd stayed on to help.

Michelle took over the running of the firm Tyrone had left to Kayla, allowing her the quiet month she'd spent "processing" his death at a treatment facility known for their discretion. In truth, her friend had driven her right to the front door of the facility and left her there with a promise to return in thirty days.

Like clockwork, Michelle showed up at Briarwood when the month was over and greeted Kayla with an anger-meltingly warm hug and an enormous peanut-butter-cup, ice-cream blender from the nearest dairy bar.

Kayla had been forced to admit her friend had been right on a number of levels before Michelle agreed to hand over the treat. And nothing had ever felt—or tasted—so good to her.

Since she'd found her husband murdered, Kayla had taken to eating her feelings. Her sweet tooth had been nearly insatiable. She'd put on ten pounds and was reduced to selecting the day's outfit from the section of her closet comprised of Lycra-enhanced ensembles, but she couldn't quite bring herself to care too much about her appearance.

She felt good.

Healthy.

Grounded.

Her newfound peace of mind also came with a side order of survivor's guilt, but she had a therapist to help her work through those issues.

She was alive and well, working herself up to taking over the empire the man she'd loved had entrusted to her. She didn't have time to worry about a few extra pounds.

Michelle even had the nerve to tell her she looked better with the extra weight. But she didn't have her friend's beautifully rounded curves, nor had she been so fashionably thin the gains weren't noticeable.

Therefore, she walked the half-mile to the end of the drive and back again each day. Pumping her arms slightly faster, she vowed to make the mostly uphill trek back at the same pace. The house had a home gym, but she liked being outdoors. Walking the driveway and wandering the sprawling house counted as cardio as far as Kayla was concerned. And, since she was never going back to the house where her husband was killed, the lake house would be her home base until she got her legs under her.

Continuing to twirl the stem of the leaf between her thumb and middle finger, she rounded the bend in the road leading to the gate. The heavy old wrought iron stood stalwart between her and the outside world. The mailbox was built into one of the brick pillars that supported the ostentatious gate with its stylized *P* worked into its curlicues.

The walk was an exercise in futility on top of being exercise for the body. There was rarely anything but junk mail in the box. The need to have mail delivered to their remote lake house was a relic from the days when Tyrone's father refused to leave town without every available means of communication.

In the years since she'd married Ty, Kayla never thought to check the box. The caretaker who came by once a week to do routine maintenance gathered anything of importance and forwarded it all to the PP&W offices. But the day Michelle had driven her back here, she'd spotted the mailbox as they waited for the gate to open and decided the walk down the drive and back daily would do her some good.

A few yards from the gate, she stopped, reached into a neatly trimmed boxwood hedge and lifted the cover on a concealed keypad. When Tyrone first showed her the hidden control panel, she'd laughed. It seemed like one of those ridiculous, rich-people things to do—hiding an unsightly keypad in a hedge. Now each time she reached into the shrub, she heard his voice reciting the code and repeating it over and over.

"Eight-six-three-seven," she whispered to his memory.

Kayla had never considered herself a particularly spiritual person. She didn't get all woo-woo about being in touch with her late husband. She missed talking to him. The scent of him. Sharing her thoughts with a man who appreciated her mind as well as her body.

But he was gone, and in the past month she'd done her best to come to terms with that distasteful fact. If her stint in rehab had taught her anything, it was how to live in the here and now.

Stepping back, she smirked as the iron gate began its slow swing on creaking hinges. This was all part of the routine. And routines were important these days. Routines kept her tethered.

With the gate standing wide open, she walked around to the other side of the column and pulled the latch on the metal box. She stuck her hand in to be sure she'd gathered everything. An office-supply company was pushing a special on copy paper and there was a notice from the marina where Tyrone had the family's boats serviced and stored for the winter.

She hadn't thought much about boats lately. She certainly hadn't thought about going out on the lake. Tyrone's son, Trey, had been under indictment when they were killed. He'd been awaiting trial in the death of a young woman who'd either fallen or been pushed overboard while riding on Trey's boat.

Another unsolved death.

Michelle had been defending Trey on behalf of Powers, Powers & Walton, the firm Ty's father had founded. Kayla was relieved Michelle had agreed to act as her counselor after the murders, and grateful when she agreed to take leave from the FBI in order to stay on and keep the firm on an even keel until Kayla could come back at full strength.

The time had come.

Kayla expected to step into the role of managing partner at Powers, Powers & Walton. She also planned to do her level best to convince Michelle to give up her work with the Bureau and stay on at PP&W.

She was fairly certain she might be able to recruit Lieutenant Ethan Scott, the detective assigned to investigate the deaths of her husband and stepson, as an ally in her campaign to convince Michelle to stay. There was something going on between them, even if her friend had remained frustratingly reticent about the relationship under her cross-examination.

Kayla stooped to check the box one last time to make sure she'd gathered every last circular. As she straightened, she heard a loud pop behind her. She spun around as a hot gust of wind whooshed by her and a sharp searing pain ripped through her left arm.

"What the—"

She looked down and saw the sleeve of her shirt was torn. Blood seeped through the fabric. Pressing the hand holding the sale flyers over the hole, she scanned the area on the opposite side of the lake road.

But she saw no movement.

Not surprising. The whole area was heavily wooded. A good chunk of the land was owned by the Powers Family Trust, but a number of acres were leased out to hunting clubs. It wouldn't be unheard of for a bullet to go astray in these woods, but she was fairly sure the noise she heard had not come from a rifle. No. A handgun. Someone had fired a handgun out here. At her.

She dropped the junk mail, then held her injured arm as she ran back through the gate.

She grimaced as she poked at the control panel concealed in the hedge with fingers trembling and smeared with her own blood.

"Come on," she whispered, her voice shaking nearly as much as her hand.

She felt a trickle of blood run down her arm, and she jabbed at the button again.

"Come on, come on, come on," she repeated through clenched teeth as the ancient gate finally swung into motion. Then, realizing the rusty iron bars would provide no cover, she wedged herself into the neatly trimmed boxwood hedge, hoping it might conceal her as well as it did the control panel for the gate.

Her mind whirred while she waited to hear the solid *ka-thunk* of the gate latch falling into place.

She'd been foolish to refuse the offer of having a police officer on scene. With Tyrone and Trey's murderer still at large, both the Arkansas State Police and the Carroll County Sheriff's Department had offered protection. But she'd turned them down, thinking she'd be safe at the lake house. Who would come all the way out here to take a shot at her?

"Someone who doesn't want me coming back to Bentonville," she muttered under her breath.

She leaned out of the hedge, impervious to the sharp pokes and jabs from the shrub.

She heard a motor start and prayed the damn gate would latch already.

Tempted to run out and shove it closed, she froze when an engine revved. She hadn't even had time to sink back into the shrub when a pickup truck roared up the road, slowing as it passed the gate.

Biting her lip to keep from making a noise, she stared hard at the vehicle and tried to take in as much as she could. New. An import. No rusted-out Chevy or Ford for this hunter. She squinted, trying to get a look at the driver. But the sun glinted off the windshield, and all she could make out was the shadow of a man.

Something about him was breathtakingly familiar. This was a man she knew. But from where?

And why would he shoot at her?

Try as she might, Kayla couldn't get her brain to engage.

The gate finally clanged to a close, and the sound seemed to startle the driver into action. He cut the wheel hard to the left and peeled away from the driveway, sending up a spray of loose gravel when he caught the shoulder of the county road. She ran back to the gate and craned her neck but could not get a clear view of the license plate.

The vehicle was either a dusty black or dark gray.

Dual rear tires. These details might help make it easier to spot here, where the locals would disparage anything not made by an American car company.

The moment the sound of the truck's engine faded away she took off and started up the drive. She kept her head low and stuck close to the tree line until she knew she was around the bend. The gate would stop a car, but it would prove no deterrent if her assailant decided to pull over and hoof it through the woods. She needed to get to the house.

Who was he?

Recognition niggled at her, but she didn't take time to puzzle it out. The parcel of the lakefront real estate the first Tyrone Powers had snatched up not long after the US Army Corps of Engineers dammed the White River was massive and largely unfenced. And the waterfront was entirely unprotected. Table Rock Lake's many inlets and hidden coves could provide the perfect access point for anyone who wanted to get to the house.

The house she'd left completely unlocked.

What had she been thinking?

Kayla trotted along the edge of the drive, thankful the property sloped down toward the waterfront. She slowed to a fast walk when she caught sight of the turreted roofline of the pseudo castle Tyrone Powers Senior had built as a testament to his wealth. Feeling slightly safer away from the road, she patted the side pocket of her yoga pants, then grimaced.

No phone.

A glance down at the bloody streaks she'd left on the fabric added insult to injury. She gritted her teeth and allowed herself a soft hiss as she covered the wound with her hand again. Steeling herself against the pain, she flexed the fingers of her left hand to confirm the arm was still in working order despite the fire radiating from her bicep.

When she entered treatment, she'd willingly handed over her cell phone, knowing Michelle or Lieutenant Scott could get ahold of her whenever necessary. In the three days since she checked herself out, Kayla had almost forgotten what it was like to check her phone constantly, and now made a conscious effort to move about in the world without it.

In the weeks she'd been away, she'd become accustomed to going without her phone. Life without a constant source of communication proved to be refreshing,

Following the arrest of Harold Dennis they'd been inundated by both local and national media. Harold was believed to be the mastermind behind a Ponzi scheme dedicated to funneling money into a political-action committee used to fund Senator William Powers's campaigns. With charges of fraud and money laundering pending, and proof Harold had a private jet at his disposal, the attorney who'd once been her husband's mentor was being held in the Benton County Correctional Facility while various government agencies battled it out to see which one would get to charge him first.

The ties to Senator William Powers and allegations of possible campaign-finance violations were chum to the media frenzy. The arrest compounded the notoriety gained by an unsolved double homicide and the possible murder—or at best negligent homicide—of a local young woman, Mallory Murray.

All in all, the Powers family had become lightning rods for news stories guaranteed to make readers say "No way!" as they gobbled up the details.

The stress of being left in charge of the family firm, her grief over the loss of her husband and the trauma of being the one to find his body had nearly broken her. Nearly, but not quite, thanks to her best friend. Within a week, she was downing more than a bottle of wine a night. Barely ten days after Harold's arrest, Michelle and the ever-present Ethan Scott staged a sort of intervention.

Thank goodness.

But she regretted her insistence on staying isolated and disconnected at the moment.

Hustling up the lane, she focused on the front door. She couldn't think too hard about the pain in her arm or possible blood loss.

"Fool, fool, fool," she murmured.

What made her think she was safe here when Tyrone hadn't been safe in their own home in the middle of town? Someone could have walked right in while she was out strolling along picking up leaves. She might as well have left a pie baking on the windowsill and rolled out a red carpet for a welcome mat.

Still, instinct told her inside was better than outside. Besides, she needed to call for help.

"Get inside, get inside," she whispered to herself.

Kayla stumbled over the threshold and made a beeline for the back of the house. Her cell would be in her purse, but she wouldn't bother trying to locate it now. Instead, she headed for the ancient phone mounted on the kitchen wall.

She'd teased Tyrone for insisting on keeping a landline connected, but cellular service could be sporadic in the area. Aside from the wall-mounted handset in the kitchen, there was a multiline speakerphone in Ty's former office. It was another relic of his father's days at the helm, but Ty could never bring himself to cut the cord.

Chest heaving, she snatched the kitchen phone from its cradle and fumbled it with fingers sticky with drying blood. She managed to press the numbers 911, then raised the receiver to her ear. The call didn't go through right away and the silence on the other end shot a fresh burst of panic through her. What if the person who'd shot her had cut the phone lines?

Gripping the receiver, she lunged for her handbag. But to her relief, the call connected at last and the line began to ring.

"Carroll County emergency," a woman with a thick drawl answered. "Police, fire or medical emergency?"

"Uh…" Kayla hesitated, her brain freezing. The only thing she could rule out for certain was fire. "Not fire," she blurted.

"Police or medical?" the dispatcher repeated.

"Both," Kayla said, her voice a hoarse whisper.

She gritted her teeth as her breaths came short and fast. Her vision blurred around the edges. She blinked and tried to lock in on something solid. Immovable. But everything was getting fuzzy, and she couldn't force her gaze to light on any one item.

"I need help," she said weakly "I've been—"

Her knees turned to jelly, and she grabbed the side of the kitchen island in a vain attempt to stay upright. But it was no good. She'd reached out with her left arm and a fresh lightning bolt of pain brought her to her knees.

"What kind of help, ma'am?" the dispatcher replied. "Ma'am?"

Kayla tried to form words, but the only ones that sprang to mind were so incomprehensible to her she couldn't make them come out.

"Ma'am?" the dispatcher said sharply, and Kayla let out a soft moan. "Ma'am? Stay with me," the dispatcher implored. "What can I do for you?"

"I've been—" Kayla tried to take a deep breath, but her chest felt like a cartoon coyote had dropped an anvil on it and blackness narrowed her blurry vision to pin points.

"Shot," she said at last. "I've been shot."

As the darkness closed in, she thought of the pregnancy tests she'd planned to purchase when she went into Eureka Springs. "Please, please," she whispered, her hand moving to cover her stomach as consciousness slipped out of her grasp.

Chapter Two

Kayla woke up in a room so preternaturally white, for a moment she thought it might be heaven. This antiseptic, blinding room was not painted one of the many shades of white the decorator had used in the sumptuous living room of her Bentonville house.

A beautiful house she'd never live in again.

This was not the house where Ty had been killed. The thought gave her a modicum of relief. But where was she now?

An overhead light glared down at her. She squeezed her eyes shut against the pain, but the brightness seared through to the inside of her eyelids, turning them a glowing orange. For a second, she wondered if she'd passed out at the dentist's office, but then she heard the blip of a machine and felt the squeeze of a blood-pressure cuff on her right arm.

"She's coming around," a brisk female voice said from somewhere behind her.

Coming around. Kayla wondered what the words were supposed to mean. She hadn't agreed to any of this. She closed her eyes again, wishing herself back into the oblivion, but then another voice broke through.

"Mrs. Powers?"

She flinched but didn't open her eyes. Kayla didn't recognize this woman's voice, either, and she wasn't entirely certain she wanted to give up her identity so readily. Something prickled at the back of her mind.

Danger.

Crack.

Shot.

At last, her eyes flew open. She found a blond woman with a stethoscope draped around her neck peering down at her, her own eyes narrowed with focus.

"Mrs. Powers?" she asked again, but the use of her name was more statement than inquisition.

Kayla returned her stare. "Who are you?"

"I'm Dr. Michaelson. You're in Emergency at Eureka Springs Hospital. Do you remember how you came to be here?"

"Nine-one-one," Kayla croaked as a flood of memory washed over her.

Shot.

Crack.

Danger.

Was this woman going to help her? She gave her head a shake to clear it, but a sharp lancing pain raced from the back of her scalp down to her neck and radiated through her body. The doctor placed a gentle hand on her arm to still her.

Kayla grimaced. "What happened?"

"We think you hit your head when you passed out. The EMT said it looked like you might have banged it against the corner of a cabinet."

"Passed out," Kayla repeated. Had she been drunk?

No. Not drunk. No drinking. Hurt. She closed her eyes. "Hurts."

"Yes," the doctor confirmed. "You were injured. Do you remember calling emergency?"

She made a noise she hoped passed for an affirmative, because speaking and nodding were proving to be equally disagreeable. Bile churned in her stomach as flashes of the trek back up her driveway played through her mind.

Shot.

The conclusion ricocheted around in her head like her assailant had pulled the trigger on it. She'd been shot in the arm. But she couldn't feel her arm. Had they taken it off? She wanted to open her eyes to check, but the second she tried to move her head, the pain came rushing back on a wave of nausea. She squeezed her eyes shut and managed a whispered reply. "Shot."

"Yes." She could hear Dr. Michaelson moving about the small space. "It appears you were shot in the left arm. Do you know how it happened?"

"Mail," Kayla replied, grimacing at the discomfort the single word unleashed.

"A male shot you?" the doctor asked, moving closer again.

Kayla chanced a peek through slit eyelids. "Yes. No," she corrected. "Can someone turn off the light?"

She heard a *click*, and the searing orange glow behind her eyelids dimmed. She exhaled but couldn't bring herself to open her eyes quite yet.

"I was getting the mail, but the person who shot at me was male. M-a-l-e," she added for clarity. The moment the letters left her lips, she began to doubt she'd selected the correct homonym. "As in male man." She gritted her teeth again as her word choice registered. "Male as in a human male," she corrected. "Not a mailman."

"I see."

Kayla cracked an eyelid and saw the doctor glancing up at someone on the other side of the room. She wanted to turn her head, but the pain stopped her. She sucked in a sharp breath, then asked breathlessly, "Who's over there?"

"Deputy Forester, ma'am." The response came from a nervous-sounding young man. "Carroll County Sheriff's Department. I responded to your call along with the EMTs from the Beaver Township Volunteer Fire Department."

"I see," Kayla said softly. "Thank you."

He shifted uncomfortably, then responded. "My pleasure to help, ma'am. Now, so I'm clear, the person who shot at you was a man, but not a mailman. Am I correct, ma'am?" he asked in his soft drawl.

"Correct."

"Deputy, if you don't mind waiting a few more minutes to interview Mrs. Powers, I'd like to go through a few routine tests with her and maybe help her get a little more comfortable," Dr. Michaelson interjected.

"Of course." The young man sounded abashed. "I'll step outside?"

The doctor nodded. "Yes, please. And I know the drill—none of the good pain meds until you've taken her statement."

"Thank you, ma'am, um, I mean, doctor," he corrected.

"A nurse will be out to get you as soon as we're finished in here."

Kayla let her eyes slide shut again as the metal rings holding the curtain surrounding them rang out. She took three long, careful breaths, releasing each one as gently as she could. Doing her utmost to avoid moving too much.

"Mrs. Powers?" Dr. Michaelson said gently.

"I'm awake," Kayla responded. "But can I keep my eyes shut for now? My head is killing me."

The doctor murmured something to her nurse. "We can give you some analgesics if you think you can keep them down."

"Yes. Thank you."

The doctor adjusted the blood-pressure cuff on her arm. Kayla felt the cool press of a stethoscope in the crook of her arm. "I'm going take your vitals, but then I'm afraid I'll need you to open your eyes when we do the cognitive exam, okay?"

"Okay," Kayla replied.

Wincing, she submitted to the thermometer under her tongue and the squeezing of her arm from the inflating cuff. She assumed the steady *beep-beep-beep* of the machine behind her was driven by the pulse monitor clipped to her index finger. She focused on keeping her breaths as even as she could while they noted her readings, but she couldn't help dreading the moment they asked her to open her eyes again. She'd been shot in the arm, not the head. How hard did she fall?

"Okay, then," the doctor said as the pressure from the cuff released and the stethoscope was removed. "You can keep them closed for a minute more. Marcy's going to get you an ice pack and some ibuprofen."

"God bless Marcy," Kayla whispered.

She could hear the smile in the doctor's voice when she responded. "I say the exact same thing several times a day."

"Come on now. Y'all are going to make me blush," the efficient nurse replied. "Back in a sec."

Kayla chanced opening an eyelid and allowed herself a soft groan. The woman standing on the other side of her bed was short, unsmiling. She wasn't plump so much as perfectly rounded. Some women had the good fortune to have all their body weight distributed evenly. Like her friend Michelle, the stranger in the pale blue scrubs looked like a cartoon pinup girl.

A cartoon pinup girl who not only had a license to practice law, but also a badge and a gun to go with it. She needed to call Michelle.

"I need to make a call," she said.

"Sure. In a minute," the doctor said distractedly.

Kayla was mustering the energy to push, when the curtain parted and a nurse she assumed was Marcy reappeared. She gulped the pills given to her in a plastic cup, swallowing them without water, but took a grateful sip when offered. She blinked once, twice, then sighed as Marcy gingerly slid the gel pack she'd activated to the base of Kayla's skull.

"Marry me," Kayla said with a tight half-smile.

"I doubt your husband would appreciate you dumping him for a girl with a cold pack," the nurse said with a teasing smile.

"My husband is dead," Kayla said, letting her eyes fall shut again.

A heavy blanket of awkwardness fell over the room. Kayla didn't need to open her eyes to know she'd wiped the sassy smile right off the other woman's face. But Marcy was no pushover for emotion, and she obviously wasn't the kind of woman who let embarrassment overtake good manners. "I am sorry to hear."

"He was killed," Kayla said in a voice as rough as sandpaper.

She opened her eyes again in time to see Marcy draw in on a sharp intake of breath, even though she was wearing a mask. Sugarcoating the truth wouldn't help. She had to make these women aware that she—and they, by association—might be in peril.

Kayla forced herself to look up directly into the doctor's concerned gaze. "He was shot. In our home. In Bentonville."

"I see," Dr. Michaelson said quietly.

"Do you want me to ask the deputy to come back in?" Marcy asked without missing a beat.

Kayla wanted to shake her head, but she couldn't work up the strength. "No. Not yet. I need my phone. There's a lieutenant with the Arkansas State Police who's working the case," she informed them. "Ethan Scott."

"I'll give the deputy Lieutenant Scott's name," Marcy promised. "As for your phone, let me go check to see what the EMTs brought in with you. They would have looked for ID. They may have grabbed your whole purse."

The curtain swished shut behind her, and Kayla allowed her eyelids to slide shut again. "You may want to ask the deputy to stay nearby," she said, knowing the doctor hadn't moved one millimeter from where she'd been a moment before.

"I have no doubt Marcy has already given Deputy Forester more instructions than any man could want," she replied evenly.

"How bad is my arm?" Kayla asked, her voice shaky.

"Not bad at all."

"I can't feel it," she noted.

"The magic of a local anesthetic. I sewed you up as best I could, but it's a gouge of a flesh wound. Like a deep scrape, which can hurt like the devil."

"Like getting a bad paper cut. Might as well lop the whole hand off," Kayla said quietly.

"Exactly. Sometimes the nonfatal wounds hurt the most."

Kayla needed this dark oblivion a few minutes longer. "Pretty profound, Doctor," she said quietly.

The other woman placed a hand on her shoulder. "Rest for a few minutes. I'll speak to the deputy. Maybe he can reach out to your lieutenant, and you can answer all their questions at once."

Kayla felt one corner of her mouth twitch up involuntarily. "He's not my lieutenant," she said with a rueful little smile. "But his and my best friend Michelle Fraser's numbers should both be programmed into my phone."

"Any family we should contact?"

Kayla's throat ran dry. She licked her lips, hoping she could force out the sad syllable trapped there. "No. Michelle can handle everything."

The doctor gave her wrist a squeeze, then stepped

away from the exam table. "I hear that. As long as you've got a best girlfriend, you've got everything you need to get through this."

"Not only is she my emergency contact, but she's also my attorney."

"I've already made a note of her name," the other woman assured her. "Rest for a few minutes if you can."

When she woke, Kayla couldn't say whether minutes or hours had passed. The moment she'd been left alone, she'd fallen into a deep sleep. The kind too thick for dreams. Thank God. She awoke to find herself peering into the concerned blue eyes of her best friend.

"Hey," she croaked.

"Hey," Michelle responded. "Guess who's not allowed to go to the lake house by herself anymore?" she said in a voice tremulous with emotion.

"I'm going to go out on a limb and say it's me," Kayla rasped.

"Bingo."

"Is Ethan with you?"

"Of course. I sent him to get us coffee. You were pretty zonked out, and the poor deputy out there is drooping."

"Someone shot me."

Michelle gripped the rail on the side of the bed. "I heard a rumor."

"The thing is, I can't be exactly sure, but I can't help thinking the person I saw in the truck reminded me of someone I know."

"Have you been able to piece it together?" Michelle asked, cutting to the chase.

"I want to say it was Del," Michelle said in a strangled whisper. "Actually, I don't want to say it was, but my gut is telling me I saw Del."

Her husband's nephew. Senator William Powers's son. A man she'd once considered a friend. But that was before she'd inherited the law firm his family founded.

"Did you get a good look at him?"

"No. The sunlight was glinting off the windshield. I couldn't swear to it. It's…"

"Okay." Michelle nodded once in simple acceptance.

Kayla looked over at her friend, for a moment marveling how easy the relationship between them was. She'd told Michelle nothing but the unvarnished truth from the day she walked into the house and found Tyrone and Trey dead on the sofa, and Michelle believed her.

"Do I tell Ethan?" Kayla asked, looking her friend directly in the eye.

"Why wouldn't you?" Michelle answered.

Kayla huffed a laugh. "Lawyers. Always answering a question with a question."

Michelle leaned in. "Seriously, why wouldn't you tell Ethan?"

"I didn't see his face. I can't swear to it in court. As far as I know, Del doesn't own a vehicle like the truck I saw. I have no reason to say it's him other than my gut."

She pressed her hand low on her belly, suddenly remembering she'd never taken a pregnancy test. She'd need to talk to Dr. Michaelson. Perhaps she could have her hunch confirmed before she was discharged.

"Gut instinct hasn't steered us wrong yet," Michelle

reminded her. "But if it is Del, we're going to have to be careful not to tip our hand. It's bad enough a prominent lawyer and good friend of Senator Powers has been arrested for financial crimes. It's another thing entirely if we go around accusing his only son of attempted homicide without something solid."

"I know. I'm asking you. Do we tell Ethan?"

Michelle nodded. "Yes, but maybe let it sit a bit until you feel more certain. You're shaken up now, and he'll want to go after Del. He won't do anything rash, but things are precarious at the moment."

"One way of putting it," Kayla muttered.

Her friend's eyes twinkled, but her smile was small and reassuring. "When you feel sure you can trust him."

"If you say so, then I do."

Michelle reached over and grasped the hand Kayla had pressed to her belly. Squeezing it hard, she said, "In the meantime, we want to get you some protection. We need to get you away from here." Kayla started to protest, but Michelle only squeezed her hand harder. "Don't argue with me. You know I'm right. Until we can figure out who killed Tyrone and Trey, you're not going to be safe."

"I won't be driven away."

"Your hubris is showing," Michelle said harshly. "Someone shot at you today."

"I know. I was there," Kayla replied. "But I was oblivious. Thought I was impervious. Now I know I'm a target." She met her friend's gaze and held it. "I won't let my guard down again."

"No. And even if you do, I'm making sure someone has your back."

"Michelle—"

Ethan Scott of the Arkansas State Police Criminal Investigation Division chose that moment to make his entrance.

"Knock, knock," he called from the other side of the curtain.

Michelle's face instantly lit, and Kayla found herself so enraptured by the happiness shining from her usually stoic friend's bright eyes that she failed to respond.

"Come in," Michelle said, her smile widening when he extended one of the coffee cups to her. Deputy Forester entered behind them, surreptitiously taking a sip from his own cup, then turned in a tight circle as he looked for a surface to place it on. At last, he settled for placing it on the floor.

"Mrs. Powers, are you up to making a statement now?" he asked, his expression eager as he pulled a phone from his belt.

"Are you going to record it?" Michelle stepped in, always a lawyer first.

"Since Mrs. Powers can't come in to make a statement, it's easier for me to capture everything I need for my report on audio, ma'am. If you prefer, I can type notes." He turned back to Kayla and shrugged. "I'm happy to do whatever works for you."

Kayla and Michelle shared a glance, but Kayla wasn't worried about saying anything wrong. She'd walked to her mailbox and gotten shot. If he pressed about the truck or its driver, she could give a description without naming names.

"I'm okay with recording," she replied. "Easier to do it all at once."

Ethan pulled out his phone, too, and set it beside the deputy's on a small rolling table, but he let the younger man take the lead in gathering her statement. Kayla recounted her walk to the mailbox and the routine she'd fallen into over the course of the week, but not the reasons behind it. She explained the gate setup, and what she'd found in the mailbox. Closing her eyes, she relived those moments of pain and confusion. And when the deputy asked her for any description she could give for her assailant, she gave him exactly what she remembered seeing.

When she finished, Deputy Forester thanked her for her time, wished her a speedy recovery and left with a promise to stay in touch with her and with the state police.

Michelle stepped over to the curtain, presumably to be sure they would be alone for at least a few minutes. Kayla took the opportunity to close her eyes again, but whatever rest she thought she might get was quickly preempted by Ethan Scott.

"Don't go back to sleep," he ordered in a tone so commanding she couldn't have kept her eyes shut with superglue.

She glared up at him. "I was only resting my eyes. I don't know if anyone told you this, Lieutenant Scott, but I have a mild concussion."

He smirked at her officious tone. They'd moved way

past formalities. "Hard to believe someone so hard-headed can be concussed."

"A thick skull makes the brain sloshing more damaging," Michelle said, letting the curtain fall back into place. "She thinks she can go back to the lake house."

Ethan's eyebrows rose as Michelle joined him at her bedside. They stared down at her like disapproving parents. It was enough to get her hackles up. "I know I can go back to the lake house. It's mine and I am not being detained for any legal reason."

"Only logical ones," Ethan said gruffly.

"You have a concussion. You can't be left alone," Michelle began.

"You're welcome to join me for the night," Kayla responded magnanimously. "After you're done updating me on P, P and W, we can play board games and watch movies."

Rather than prickle, Michelle smiled. "An excellent plan. But we need to formulate one that extends beyond tonight."

Ethan spoke quietly. "We need to think about our next steps carefully, but I don't think we can do so without making sure you have security on you 24/7."

"I don't know if I can handle being under surveillance."

"I don't know if you have a choice," Michelle interjected.

"There's always a choice," Ethan replied smoothly. "We are asking you to make the smart one."

"I don't want a deputy parked outside my door all the time."

"I think we're beyond a patrol car as a deterrent," he said gravely. "Someone came after you, Kayla. You don't need a marked car parked outside to scare people off. You need personal protection."

"Like a bodyguard," she stated flatly.

He nodded. "Sort of. I have a friend also with the Arkansas State Police based out of Little Rock who specializes in protective services. I'm going to see if we can get him up here. Given how high-profile these cases have become, I doubt I'll get any pushback."

Gnawing her bottom lip, Kayla sighed and lowered her gaze. "Who is this friend?"

"His name is Special Agent Ryan Hastings. He used to be CID at Little Rock. Now he's a sergeant in the Executive Protection Division."

She sniffed, shifting him a peevish look. "Only a sergeant? Shouldn't I get someone who's at least officer-grade?"

Ethan smirked. "Different division, different rankings, but trust me, you want this guy on your side. He's protected presidents, celebrities, foreign dignitaries… even your brother-in-law."

Kayla and Michelle's gazes met and held at the mention of Bill Powers. She knew she had to tell Ethan about her suspicions regarding Del.

"I gave Deputy Forester my description of the guy in the truck, but what I didn't say is, I think—" she paused and held up the finger with the pulse oximeter attached for emphasis "—*think*, the person driving it might have been Del Powers."

To his credit, Ethan didn't flinch.

"Did you see him clearly enough to testify?"

"No."

"This is nothing more than an impression?"

"My gut feeling. At first, I couldn't place him. Couldn't figure out what was familiar, but when I woke up, his name popped into my head."

"Noted," Ethan said with a brisk nod. "I'm going to step out and make a couple of calls." He turned to Michelle. "Try to talk her into coming back into town. The lake house is too isolated and not at all secure."

"We can argue later?" She turned to Michelle. "Would you send Dr. Michaelson back in? I need to speak to her about my follow-up care."

The minute they'd left, she ran her hand over her still-flat belly, wondering but afraid to hope her suspicions would play out. And she figured she couldn't ask for a better time or place to get answers. If she was indeed pregnant, she would have to give in to some of Michelle and Ethan's demands.

She sighed as Marcy poked her head in. "Dr. Michaelson is with another patient. Did you need something, hon?"

Wetting her lips, Kayla nodded, then beckoned the nurse to come closer. In a voice so low she was certain it wouldn't carry, she whispered, "Is there a way you can run a pregnancy test for me?"

The nurse blinked, gripping the rail on the side of the bed as she reared back. "A pregnancy test?" she repeated. "Oh, honey, we do that as a matter of routine when we have an unconscious female." Her brow crinkled. "Did you not know?"

Kayla shook her head, a hot prickle of tears stinging her eyes and clogging her throat. "No," she croaked.

"Well, sugar, you are indeed pregnant." She consulted the tablet she held, tilting her head as she looked for the information. "Do you have an idea of possible conception date?"

Kayla shook her head, this time impervious to the pain. She searched her memory, trying to remember exactly how long it had been since she and Ty last made love. A week before his death? Two?

"Months," she said at last. "More than two."

Nurse Marcy looked up sharply. "Oh," she said softly, her mouth rounding with the shape of the sound. "I see."

"My husband has been gone nearly two months," Kayla said, allowing the tears to fall. "Maybe a couple weeks before he was—" She couldn't finish the sentence.

"You'll need to see your ob-gyn as soon as you get back to town, then. They'll probably want to do an ultrasound, too."

Kayla let go, letting the sobs rack her body as her mind whirled. How much wine had she drunk in those months? Her doctor had given her a sedative the night she found Ty and Trey. Would it hurt the baby? Had she somehow managed to mess this up already?

Marcy was handing over the tissue box when Michelle reappeared with a jangle of curtain rings. "Okay, I'm going— What is it? What happened?" she demanded, dividing her piercing blue glare between Kayla and poor Marcy. "What's wrong?"

"My head," Kayla gasped before the nurse could say a word.

She and Marcy shared a long look before she shifted her attention back to her friend. Kayla wasn't ready to tell anyone yet. She needed more time to process. A chance to plan. She'd tell Michelle and Ethan soon, but for this moment, she wanted to hold this knowledge close to her heart. At least until a doctor could tell her everything was okay.

"My arm hurts, too. I got shot, remember?" she said, focusing on Michelle again.

"I'll go process your discharge paperwork," Nurse Marcy murmured, and with a swish of the curtain, she was gone.

Chapter Three

Ryan Hastings wasn't particularly thrilled by the prospect of babysitting a socialite, but these days he'd do about anything to get out of the office. When he'd been a special agent for the Criminal Investigation Division, he was always on the go. But then the opportunity to transfer to Executive Protection Division came up, and it seemed like a great opportunity. In a lot of ways, it was. But the job also came with a ton of downtime.

Arkansas wasn't exactly a hot destination for visiting celebrities and dignitaries.

Now, he'd torn his ACL while protecting the head football coach from a particularly exuberant scrum of students and players following a stunning victory. He didn't blame them for storming the field. Nor did he resent being injured in the line of duty. He'd done his level best to protect the state's highest paid public employee, he thought with a smirk. He simply hated being desk-bound.

As he drove the long stretch of interstate west out of Little Rock, he wondered if most people in the United States realized their highest-paid public officials weren't governors or senators, or any of the people who made the laws who govern their land, but rather the men who led their collegiate teams into battle each week.

He winced as he drew up his left leg and planted his foot on the floorboard. Sitting for a three-hour car trip was never pleasant, but flexing and straightening his leg periodically helped. He'd switched off the radio an hour outside of Little Rock, tired of searching for something he found palatable. With nothing left to do, he activated the voice command and placed a call to his old friend, Lieutenant Ethan Scott.

"You on your way?" Ethan asked by way of greeting.

"Yep. Still a couple hours out," Ryan responded. "Give me the skinny on this whole thing again."

"Ah, you're bored," Ethan replied.

"Radio wasteland." He stretched his neck. "Entertain me."

He'd done his homework, of course. Aside from the official case filings on the charges pending against Trey Powers at the time of his murder, and the ongoing investigation into who had shot both Trey and his father, Tyrone, he's also done a deep dive into the media coverage.

The story was sensational. National news outlets had picked it up and couldn't seem to let it go. Mostly they seemed to be amazed anyone outside of New York or Los Angeles had any kind of real money, power or influence. Those metropolitan worlds were so insular they couldn't imagine the scheming going on beneath the seemingly bucolic settings of America's small towns and rural cities.

"Once upon a time there was a man named Tyrone

Delray Powers. Old Tyrone bought up a good chunk of hill country in northwest Arkansas," Ethan began.

"Seems like a dubious investment," Ryan replied dryly. "Must have had some insider information."

"Seems he probably did, doesn't it? Only a couple years later, the US Army Corps of Engineers came in and dammed up the White River, flooded the valleys and created the lakes we now know as Bull Shoals, Beaver Lake and Table Rock Lake."

"Three of my favorite places on earth," Ryan interjected.

"Same. Anyhow, old Tyrone had amassed a fairly substantial fortune in real-estate speculation. He made some friends who turned out to be successful, too. One who started a massive chain of discount stores you may have seen scattered around."

"Birds of a feather," Ryan said.

"They do indeed flock together. Our friend Tyrone was the industrious type. Aside from all his real-estate wheeling and dealing, he put himself through law school and opened one of the area's most prestigious law firms, setting himself up to be the guy all those birds came to when they pooped on the wrong person."

"Okay, spare me the bird jokes," Ryan interrupted.

"Anyhow, Tyrone sent his two boys back east to law school so they could rub shoulders with more—sorry—feathered friends, then bring those connections back to their sweet little setup in a mountain town they helped put on the map."

"Those two boys would be Tyrone Junior and Senator Bill Powers," Ryan concluded.

"Bingo. Daddy also helped one of his good buddies by letting him buy his favorite nephew a partnership in the firm."

"And the nephew would be the Walton in Powers, Powers and Walton."

"Yes. Some might have called him a poor relation, but not anymore," Ethan said with a chuckle. "Like all these guys, he managed to make his way up in the world."

"He's a judge now, right?" Ryan said, lining up players in his mind.

"Correct."

"If he's a judge, doesn't partnership in a law firm create some kind of conflict of interest?"

"Well, it might seem fishy to an outside observer, but let's not forget we're dealing with what was a fairly small community up until the last decade or two. When he took the bench, he withdrew his partnership in the firm."

"Ah, America. The land of a chicken in every pot and a finger in every pie," Ryan said wryly.

"Exactly."

"And folks around there didn't mind?"

"Are you kidding me? Folks around here love these people. Up until a few months ago, they wanted them to come to every event, kiss their babies and toss hundred-dollar bills into the air when they left." Ethan hesitated for a second. "We think we see the haves versus the have-nots down in Little Rock, but I promise you the dividing line up here's a whole lot more…marked."

Ryan thrummed his fingers on the steering wheel as the tires hummed below him. "We don't think there's any chance whoever did this was simply somebody who is tired of not getting their slice of the pie?"

"It's possible," Ethan said fairly. "We haven't ruled it out, but there aren't any other suspects. P, P and W did not specialize in the sort of law that puts people in regular contact with the more troubled parts of the local society. At least, not the way we think of as troubled. I'm sure these people have their own set of worries, but they mainly deal with corporate law. White-collar stuff. As they say in the legal community, a white-shoe law firm."

"What's that supposed to mean?"

"I don't actually know, but I'm assuming it means something to do with wearing shoes so clean and white they wouldn't dare trek through the muck."

"Gotcha." Ryan immediately formed a picture in his mind of a bunch of white-suited, white-shoed Gatsby types tiptoeing their way across a plush lawn, croquet mallets in hand. "And the widow Powers?"

"Kayla?" Ethan chuckled. "I think you're going to be pleasantly surprised."

"How so?"

"She wasn't exactly what I expected when I came into town. I imagine she won't be what you have in mind, either," Ethan said cryptically.

"How do you know what I have in mind?" Ryan challenged.

"I think we all pretty much have the same image in our heads when we imagine the much-younger second wife of a rich man."

"A Hollywood stereotype," Ryan said, a dark edge creeping into his voice.

Ethan didn't know—couldn't have known—Ryan's own mother had been the second wife of a wealthy man. But his past wasn't relevant to this case.

"How is she going to surprise me?"

"Kayla is bright. Sharp. She was an attorney at the firm when she married Tyrone."

"Gold digger?" Ryan asked, his tone flat.

"Some people say so, of course, but I don't think so. She got there on her own and doesn't seem to want what's been left to her. I think they had an actual relationship. A real marriage with all the ups and downs. She's shockingly forthcoming, so I'm sure she'll tell you herself that their relationship was in a bit of a rocky patch at the time of Tyrone's death."

"What kind of rocky patch?"

"Nothing dramatic. She said some of the newness had worn off and he didn't seem as interested in her as he had once been. He had his own set of problems with the son, Trey, and the charges against him."

"I read the news stories. This family sounds like a bit of a mess," Ryan commented, knowing he was greatly understating the dynamics at play.

"Aren't all families?"

"Maybe," Ryan conceded. His certainly was.

"I like Kayla," Ethan admitted gruffly. "She's a straight shooter." Then, as if realizing what he said, he rushed to clarify. "Not an actual shooter, but I mean—"

"I get it. She doesn't bother with a lot of filler," Ryan concluded for him.

"Exactly. She's an attorney. Thinks like one. Strategic, factual, logical…"

Ethan paused, and Ryan wondered what was hanging up his old friend when it came to describing this woman.

"Cold fish?" he said, hazarding a guess.

"No," Ethan answered. "Definitely not."

Ryan sensed a hesitation. "But?"

"I know she won't mind me telling you, because it's probably going to be the first topic she brings up, but she recently came out of a thirty-day treatment program."

Ryan spotted a sign for the exit that would take him north over the Boston Mountains and into the Ozarks. He signaled a lane change then settled in, his gaze fixed on the exit in the distance. The road would take him closer to this straight-shooting woman with addiction problems, a big, fat pile of money and someone taking shots at her.

"Pills?"

"Booze," Ethan corrected. "Wine, actually."

"Any other issues I need to be aware of? Disruptive behavior? Violent tendencies?"

"Nothing along those lines," Ethan assured him. "I would assess her more as a woman with too much time on her hands and not enough attention from her husband. She's an introvert. Tends to hole up. Maybe a strong desire to numb herself comes along with the urge to hide."

"Because she needs to be insulated from all the money and power she married into?" Ryan asked, a note of snark entering his tone as he coasted onto the exit ramp.

"More like she needed to blunt the edges of the slings and arrows aimed at the replacement wife," Ethan replied evenly.

Ryan's shoulders dropped and he exhaled, the sound soft and low. He knew exactly the kind of treatment Kayla Powers had likely endured as the newer, younger model. He'd watched his own mother try to navigate those treacherous waters. Watched it whittle her away to a sharp stick of a woman so afraid of making a misstep, she'd stood frozen by her husband's side, simply absorbing the vitriol so casually flung at her.

Through his teenage years, he'd watched as the loving mother he'd known cloaked all of her soft spots in armor plating. He couldn't help wondering if she missed being married to his dad. Jerry Hastings had been a moderately successful insurance agent. A middling handsome guy with dark red hair and a friendly smile. He'd been Ryan's Little League coach and helped him construct cars for soapbox derbies and ships for cardboard regattas.

He'd been killed by a drunk driver when Ryan was only thirteen years old.

For three years, Ryan had done his best to protect his mother, assuming the mantle of man of the house and taking care of her the best any teen boy could. But then, his mother had met Richard Stephenson and married him after a whirlwind courtship. Suddenly, he found himself with a stepfather he barely knew, and Ryan's services as head of the family were no longer needed.

"I'll keep an open mind," Ryan assured his old friend.

"Thank you. I didn't want you coming into this thinking anyone was trying to hide her circumstances from you."

"I appreciate the information. The more I know about what she's dealing with, the better I can plan."

"Yeah, I know." Ethan paused for a moment. "She needs someone with an objective eye. Needs you."

Ryan winced as the other man inadvertently pressed the hottest of his many hot buttons. He could never resist helping someone who needed him.

"Listen, we're going to meet you at her lake house. I'll send you a pin drop for the GPS."

"A pin drop? Is it far off the beaten path?"

"It's over on Table Rock in a remote and fairly isolated area." Ethan's response was terse. "Michelle and I have been trying to convince her to move somewhere closer to town. We're hoping hearing it from you will convince her we aren't being overprotective."

"Didn't you say the lake house was where she was shot?" he asked, incredulous.

"Yes. I told you, she's stubborn. We need backup on this, and we're counting on you to give it to us."

Ryan's phone dinged and the dash display showed the message with the GPS coordinates. He grunted and jabbed at the screen until the system rerouted him to his intended destination. "ETA—one hour, fifty-two minutes."

"Ten-four," Ethan responded. "See you soon. And thanks," he added before ending the call.

Ryan readjusted his grip on the steering wheel and his expectations of the woman he was meant to protect. From the sound of things, he wouldn't find a cowering widow waiting for him at this remote lake house. With Ethan's insider information in mind, he formulated a new strategy for how he'd approach Kayla Powers.

The drive passed quickly. Ethan hadn't been exaggerating when he said a pin drop was easier. The place was out in the middle of nowhere. He hadn't been impressed by the lack of fencing adjacent to the ancient iron gate. A gate without perimeter deterrent was a moot point. The lackluster security was a disappointment. But the lake house itself was something to see.

And the moment he stepped into the room he could tell the widow with the formidable stubborn streak was not what he expected.

He'd seen photos of her in the news coverage of the Powers family's trials and tragedies. There were her photos in the official state-police files, and dozens more polished images taken at fundraisers and parties popped up with a simple internet query. He'd read enough about her background to combine all of those snapshots with the snippets of information to form a composite of the woman he thought he was meeting.

The reality of her made far more of an impact.

He took a minute to catalog the differences as Ethan made the introductions. He recognized the woman who'd been seated beside Kayla on the sofa as the defense attorney who'd represented both Trey Powers and Kayla.

Michelle Fraser. He repeated her name to himself before he turned to make a closer inspection of his charge.

Mrs. Powers's dark blonde hair was still streaked with lighter strands, but it seemed to be a bit more subdued than in some of the photos. Her cheeks were no longer gaunt, but her eyes appeared haunted. She had on the kind of stretchy pants women wore to run errands rather than do any actual running. The oversize sweatshirt she wore was silk-screened with the University of Arkansas Razorback hog mascot.

They shook hands. "Did you go to the U of A?" he asked, even though he knew the answer from the dossier Ethan had sent to him.

"Yes. For my undergrad. I attended Yale Law for my postgrad."

Coming from most people, the last might have sounded like a boast, but Kayla Powers spoke in such a direct manner he knew instinctively she was doing nothing more than stating the facts.

He smiled and took a seat in the armchair she'd waved him toward. "Are you from Arkansas originally?"

"Yes. Born and raised outside Altus," she replied, shooting Ethan a sidelong glance. "Don't tell me you didn't direct him to the Kayla Powers Cyberpedia page."

Ethan had taken the seat on Michelle Fraser's opposite side, Ryan noted. In an instant, he realized they were together. Everything about their body language screamed intimacy. There wasn't any overtly physical contact between them, but there was definitely a charge in the air.

"I prefer to ask questions. As I get to know you, I'm able to form a strategy for protection I hope would suit you, rather than other people's impressions of you."

"Funny, your friend here," she said, gesturing to Ethan, "wanted me to tell my story rather than answer questions."

"We all have different styles," he replied with what he hoped appeared to be an easy smile. "Ethan's a big-picture guy. I like the nitty-gritty data."

His statement earned him a blooming smile from Michelle. "I keep telling him data will set us free," she said, pinning Ethan with a mock glare. "He only wants me to boil everything down to the salient points for him."

"Okay, okay," Ethan said, waving them both off. "Ry, what are your thoughts on staying here at the lake house as part of your protection plan?"

Kayla Powers rolled her eyes and stuffed her hands into the pockets of her sweatshirt as she dropped back into the plush sofa cushions. "Wow. Way to serve up the softball, Lieutenant."

"I'm pretty sure I'm not going to say anything surprising, Mrs. Powers," Ryan said, meeting the woman's gaze directly. "This house is too remote. There's only one road in and out of the area. There is a gate, but the surrounding property isn't secured. I'm assuming the shoreline isn't, either."

"Correct," Kayla Powers responded, holding his gaze.

"I'm sure you have a decent security system here, but unless you plan to stay barricaded inside the house for the unforeseen future, it would be extremely difficult to be certain you'd be safe here."

"I don't relish the idea of being terrorized into making life choices," she said coolly.

"I'd say this is more of a life-or-death choice, given the circumstances surrounding your husband's murder and what happened to you yesterday."

Her chin came up a notch and her jaw stiffened, but she didn't look away. This woman was nobody's pushover.

"Sergeant Hastings—" she began.

"Ryan," he interrupted.

"Sergeant," she repeated, cocking an eyebrow at him.

He had to smile. Ethan hadn't been wrong about the stubborn streak. "Yes, Mrs. Powers?"

She huffed softly, then gave her head a rueful shake. "Ethan and Michelle have had a full day to work on me prior to your arrival. I'm not an unreasonable woman. I'm not digging in out of sheer stubbornness," she said, sliding Ethan a narrowed side-eye. "But where do you propose I go?"

Ryan opened his hands to show her he was open to any number of options. "You could go back to Bentonville. You could go to Little Rock. Or you could leave this area entirely."

"I have a law firm to run," Kayla said briskly.

"You know I would take care of things as long as you needed me to," Michelle interjected.

"I do, but the point is, I don't need you to," Kayla argued.

"Let's not get into semantics," Michelle said, raising

a hand in surrender. "I know you don't need me to run the firm, but I would be happy to help you with it if it meant we could get you someplace I know you'll be safe. As much as we would all like to believe Harold Dennis had something to do with Tyrone and Trey's deaths, we have no proof. And given what happened yesterday, I think it's safe to say there's still somebody out there who wants to harm you."

Ryan watched as Mrs. Powers took in everything her friend said. It was clear she didn't like the crux of the message. He saw her shift her jaw, her teeth clearly on edge as she bit back whatever she wanted to say. The two women stared at one another, seemingly communicating without a word being spoken. Starting to feel a little left out, he glanced over at Ethan only to see his old friend give a helpless shake of his head.

"They've got this mind-meld thing going on," he drawled in a soft undertone.

Michelle didn't bother sparing him a glance. "We're sitting right here. We can hear you."

"I'm never sure how deep it goes when you're doing the telepathy thing," Ethan answered, his grin spreading wide.

Always a man of action, Ryan decided to jump in with both feet again. "Don't you own a house in town, Mrs. Powers?"

"I'm not going there," Kayla said, tearing her gaze away from Michelle and turning to face him again.

Only then did it occur to him the house she owned in Bentonville was likely the scene of her husband's murder.

"Okay. Perhaps we can find a rental? Something clean but modest. Unassuming," he said, casting another meaningful glance around the over-the-top surroundings. "A place no one would expect you to go."

"I wasn't born with a silver spoon in my mouth, Sergeant," she said quietly.

"No, ma'am, but you have one now. No one is going to expect you to be living in anything less than the style to which you have become accustomed. We can use preconceived notions to our advantage."

"Maybe we should rent a log cabin in the woods," she suggested with an edge of snark in her tone.

One corner of his mouth kicked up. Ethan was right in his assessment. Ryan liked her spirit. "Perhaps we should. How do you feel about mounted trophies and stuffed fish?"

"You think you're going to scare me off, but I grew up around avid sportsmen and married one as well. I'm not cowed by threats of taxidermy."

"Good to know. Here's what I suggest," he said, leaning forward and planting his elbows on his knees. "A series of short-term rentals. They can all be here in the area if you want to be in the office, but we'd spread them out between Fayetteville, Rogers, Springdale and Bentonville. I know the commute can get to be a bear if you have to go at rush hour, but since you own the firm, I'm assuming you can set your own hours if you want to be a presence in the office."

She gave him a wry smirk. "Yes, I can set my own hours."

"We'll rent houses through one of those vacation

services. Rent for a week, maybe two at a time. We can pick a couple of places in town, then shift out to one of the lakes for another week or two, whatever it takes."

"How long do you think this is going to take?"

"A question for the lieutenant," he said, glancing pointedly at Ethan. "His job is to solve your husband and stepson's murders. My job would be to keep you safe until we know we have the culprit in custody."

"A bodyguard," she said dryly.

Ryan shook his head. "A common misnomer. A bodyguard is one of those big burly boys you see pushing people through crowds of paparazzi. My job is different, ma'am. I would do it if it were necessary," he added with a shrug. "But my service here is about protection. I find strategic ways to keep you safe and out of harm's way."

"And are you good at your job?" she asked coolly.

"I believe I am," he replied. "If you'd like some references, I can provide a few for you."

Again, she lifted a single eyebrow. "Can you?"

"I can't give you their contact information outright, since all of these assignments are completed in the course of my duty as an officer of the state police, but if you're a Razorback football fan, you'll recognize the name of one of them. Heck, living so close to Fayetteville, I'd bet you've probably had dinner with the man."

Sure enough, he didn't have to name names. "You would be correct. I have had dinner with him and his wife," she confirmed. "They're lovely."

"I've also worked on details for your brother-in-law,"

he told her, figuring he'd better put it all out there so there'd be no surprises later.

"Have you?" She cast a glance at over Michelle and Ethan, then turned back to him. "What if he recognizes you?"

Ryan chuckled. "Mrs. Powers, a man learns to stand out in this particular job by knowing how to blend in. I'd bet my badge Senator Powers couldn't pick me out of a lineup."

Chapter Four

The first house Sergeant Ryan Hastings procured was a typical suburban three-bedroom house in the depths of a subdivision on the north edge of Fayetteville. It was furnished comfortably enough, even if there were a few too many signs proclaiming it a happy place and making declarations about putting family first.

When Ty had been taken from her, she believed she had no family. Now she was starting to reframe the concept. Though their friendship was still new, she felt a deep connection to Michelle. A kind of kinship she imagined she might have felt if she'd had a sister. And though Kayla had a somewhat more contentious connection with Ethan, she could see him in the role of annoyingly bossy older brother. As an only child, she used to envy the kids who complained about their siblings. Now she felt close to becoming an honorary member of the club.

Her stomach muscles clenched as a rush of hot tears threatened. Instinctively, she covered her belly with her palm, and stared out the kitchen window at the wooden play set in the fenced backyard. If she kept collecting people at this rate, she'd have more family than she knew how to handle.

"This okay?"

Ryan's voice was deep, slightly breathless and held a note of warning that tempted her to push back. To insist she couldn't stay here in this bland oasis he'd booked for them. How would he react if she refused?

"This is fine." The words were out of her mouth before she'd finished her internal debate, surprising them both.

He moved to the sliding doors off the little breakfast nook and peered out as well. Was he scoping the swing set to be sure no bad guys were lurking there?

"I know it's not what you're used to, but I made sure we were within range for food-delivery services. We won't starve," he said offhandedly.

Something about his reassuring tone rubbed her the wrong way. Did he think she was so spoiled she couldn't fry an egg?

"I grew up in a house a lot like this one," she informed him.

He turned to look at her, his expression blank, but his tone gave away his surprise. "Did you?"

She nodded. "My dad sold farm equipment, and my mom was our dentist's office manager. We didn't have live-in help." She added the last part so dryly the words practically crackled.

"I see."

"I can cook. I also clean up after myself," she informed him, turning to face him head-on. "I'm fully housebroken."

He smirked at the last bit and her stomach coiled

again. Sergeant Hastings was a handsome man. She didn't blame herself for the tiny tug of attraction she felt whenever a corner of his mouth lifted, but she was no fool. She was reasonably attractive and a soon-to-be wealthy woman, if Tyrone's will stood up to the challenges brought by his family. She was a target in at least a half dozen ways, but the one she could guard herself against was getting caught up in Ryan Hastings's gravitational pull.

"Good to know." The half-smile was gone as quickly as it had appeared, and he was back to being all business. "If you'll make a list of anything you want or need, I'll add it to mine and we'll get the essentials stocked," he said briskly.

"I can do my own shopping," she insisted.

He sighed with the gusto of a man dealing with a particularly recalcitrant two-year-old. She didn't appreciate the sigh, nor did she like the look of implacable patience he wore as he heaved it.

"I won't be held prisoner—"

But he cut her protest off with a raised hand. "You are not a prisoner, but I do think it would be nice if we tried to get at least one night's stay under our belts before we run the risk of a sighting," he said gruffly.

"No one I know comes to Fayetteville outside of football or basketball season," she insisted.

"No one? Not one person from your undergrad years hung around after the ceremony. None of your fellow alumni went on to work for the university? Maybe they stayed in town and work for other companies that were on a hiring spree at the time of your graduation?"

He asked his questions with such patent disbelief she

knew instinctively he might be better equipped with an answer to his questions than she was. "Okay, maybe, but the people who know me from after—"

"We all know what a small town this entire state is," he insisted. "You're free to hit up the megacenter if you want, but don't be surprised when word of your whereabouts gets out and we find ourselves moving." He paused, fixing her with an insultingly patient gaze. "The Powers family name has featured prominently in local or national news the past couple of months. Didn't you make the cover of a tabloid? I could've sworn I saw you in the checkout line," he persisted. "No, wait, it was here." He pulled out his phone and held it up to show a headline that read "Has the Black Widow Met Her Match?"

"What the—"

She reached for the phone, her jaw dropping as she gazed at the web page in disbelief. This was no tabloid. She was staring at the front page of Little Rock's biggest newspaper. Granted, it was the digital edition, but lack of print coverage was of little consolation. The news outlet had ceased running daily print editions years before.

"I'm giving it a C minus on the truth scale. They did say you'd been unarmed when injured, but there was definitely a tone in the reporting," he said with a dismissive shrug.

"What kind of a tone?" she asked, baffled.

"The kind that says, 'It's possible she killed her husband and stepson, so maybe whoever is taking potshots might be doing the population at large a favor?'"

She tossed his phone back at him. "Disgusting."

He caught it against his chest. "Their job is to get clicks these days. And the internet lives forever. Makes you yearn for the good old days when people would line birdcages with old newspapers."

She inhaled deeply, then let out a long and loud exhale, through her nose. "Fine. I'll make a list."

"Going to the office will make keeping your whereabouts unknown tough enough. Are you sure I can't talk you out of it?"

Typical man, she thought. He tried to take a mile when she gave an inch.

Truth be told, she wasn't sure. She, Ethan and Michelle had decided she would take another few days. Del hadn't come to the office in the weeks since Harold Dennis was arrested, but the Powers men had team players all over the firm. Both Senator Powers and his son would know the minute she stepped over the threshold at PP&W, and if Del had been the one...

Kayla bit her lip as she turned away from the yard and stalked back into the main living area of the open-concept home. With every passing hour, her gut-level suspicion of Del Powers wavered a little more. She'd learned in counseling to recognize that pervasive self-doubt often rode sidecar with addiction, but she hadn't quite mastered the art of squashing it. She chose to deflect her doubts and his worries in one quick pivot.

"How many bedrooms are there?"

"Three. The main suite is on the west side. You're welcome to take it, but I have to say I'd prefer it if we could both sleep in the same part of the house. The bedrooms on the east side aren't as large, but they look comfortable enough, and I'd keep out of your way as much as possible."

The tightness in his promise pricked holes in the thin skin of her indignation. He was here to do a job, and like it or not, it was a legitimate one. She sighed, her shoulders sagging as she moved to pull one of the tall stools out from the breakfast bar.

She couldn't blame Ryan for eying her warily as she climbed onto it and planted her chin in her palm. She cringed, then ran her hand over the bandage on her upper arm, hoping he would attribute some of her foul mood to pain from her injury, not her being a pain in the rear.

"Sorry," she said, though it rang false even to her own ears.

"I understand this isn't easy," he said, meeting her gaze directly. "If it helps any, I'm every bit as uncomfortable as you are."

Oddly enough, it did make her feel better. "You are?"

He nodded. "Of course. You and I met yesterday," he said with a laugh. "I don't usually move in with a woman so quickly."

"Ha ha," she said dryly. Then it occurred to her she knew almost nothing about this man. For all she knew he was married or had a girlfriend waiting for him back in Little Rock.

"I'm sorry," she said again. "It occurred to me I don't know anything about you. Are you married?"

He shook his head. "Divorced. A long time ago."

She chuckled. "Couldn't have been too long ago. What are you, thirty-three? Thirty-four?"

It was his turn to laugh. "I'm thirty-eight, but thanks. I got married at eighteen. Divorced a year later."

Her eyebrows shot up. "Wow. You were both so young."

"Yes. And neither of us were equipped to do much more than to play house for a few months," he said with a sad half-smile. "In the end, we actually parted on fairly good terms. My ex is remarried. Has two little boys. I ran into them at a baseball game last summer."

"Oh, wow," she said softly.

"Her husband seems like a nice enough guy. In the end, I think we all made the right choices."

"And your choice was to remain single?" she asked.

"My choice was to focus on my work as much as possible."

"To the exclusion of everything else?" she persisted.

"I'm content with my life. There aren't many people who can say the same, so I count myself as lucky." He drew out the other stool and pulled it a couple feet away to leave a good amount of space between them before taking the seat. "I should say I *was* content." He gave his left knee a hard pat. "I've been sidelined with an injury for a while. Desk jockeying is not my favorite thing."

"When Ethan called to see if you'd be interested in taking this assignment, you…"

"Packed a bag and hit the road."

Turning her head, she looked at him squarely. "Surely there has to be some kind of protocol. It sounds like there's no pecking order in the state-police organization if he can call and ask you to come up here. I mean, I have to assume you have superiors and ongoing assignments. You couldn't have simply packed a bag and hit the road," she said, tossing his words back at him.

"Mrs. Powers, you have to know by now the case involving the deaths of your husband and his son are the criminal investigation division's number-one priority at this time. If Ethan Scott told the higher-ups he needed a purple unicorn with a polka-dotted mane in order to close this case, they'd be out spray-painting a horse as we speak."

She chuckled. "There's a visual image for you. I'm never going to be able to stop picturing Ethan riding around on a purple horse with a horn stuck to its head."

He chuckled, but quickly sobered. "The fact of the matter is, you are a priority within the state-police hierarchy. Your safety is of the utmost concern to everyone involved."

"Doesn't ring true if they sent a guy with a bum knee instead of an entire SWAT team," she said with a teasing smile.

"Budgetary constraints," he returned, his tone desert-dry.

She laughed out loud. "Fair enough."

She pulled her cell phone from her hip pocket, opened her note application and started typing with her thumbs. "Are you a breakfast person?"

"I'm a breakfast, lunch and dinner person," he replied without missing a beat. "But you don't have to worry about my meals. Make a list of the things you want for yourself."

"I like to cook. It relaxes me." She looked over at him. "Easier to cook for two than for one."

"I can cook, too," he assured her.

"Good. Then we can take turns." She tapped out another entry. "I didn't use to be a breakfast person," she said, continuing to type. "But now I'm embracing the whole most-important-meal-of-the-day thing. I think part of it is a rebellion against diet culture. I feel like I've been obsessed with the scale for too much of my life."

"I think people worry too much about weight and not enough about what they're putting into their bodies," he said gruffly.

She tipped her head to the side to let him know she was listening. "How do you mean?"

"Preservatives, too many chemicals, that sort of thing."

She looked up from her phone and eyeballed him with growing curiosity. "Are you a health-food guy?"

"Not necessarily. I'm more of a real-food guy," he said, shrugging off the label.

"You mean stuff like cracking an actual egg versus pouring egg substitute from a carton?"

"Pretty much. I don't go particularly out of my way to eat organic, but I do tend to try to pick foods that haven't been all radically altered from their original state."

"Makes sense. I pretty much try to do the same thing." She typed a couple more items into the list. "But I do have some weaknesses."

"Don't we all?"

She looked up, meeting his gaze directly. "I'm thirty-seven days sober. If alcohol is one of your weaknesses, I'm going to have to ask you not to bring it into the house."

"Mrs. Powers, I'm here to protect you. Even if I were

one to imbibe, I could hardly do my job if I were impaired."

"And you take your job seriously," Kayla stated, still holding his gaze.

"Very."

"My name is Kayla," she said, dragging her attention back to the phone in her hands. "If we're going to be spending time together, there's no sense standing on formality. May I call you Ryan?"

"Of course," he replied easily.

She nodded, satisfied with the exchange, but not entirely at ease. She felt strange sharing a house with a man who was not Tyrone. Almost as if she was cheating, though she knew the notion was unfounded. Trying to shake herself out of confusing thoughts involving her late husband and the man seated nearby, she zoomed in on her shopping list again.

"Yeah, well, if you have other weaknesses you want to indulge, shout them out now, because I'm putting mine on the list."

"Let me guess," he said sarcastically. "Chocolate?"

"A stereotype." She tapped a few more keys, then turned the screen to face him. "I tend to gravitate toward the salty snacks rather than the sweet."

His eyes widened as he took in the extensive list of items she was requesting from the chip aisle. "Wow. Okay. I stand corrected."

She turned the phone back and tapped out a few last items. Then, she pulled up the contact information he'd insisted they exchange immediately following the meeting with Michelle and Ethan and shared her shopping list with him.

His phone chimed a moment later. She watched his

face as he scrolled through the wish list, but saw no sign of judgment, only mild bemusement. He glanced up and caught her staring. "Sorry," she murmured, then busied herself with a response to a text from Michelle.

Del was still boycotting the office, but according to her tech-savvy friend, he'd been logging into the firm's server daily.

You'd think he'd have figured out you know the computer stuff, Kayla texted.

The dots indicating an incoming message appeared. Kayla did her best to keep her eyes glued to her own phone but couldn't help sneaking peeks at the man beside her as he typed on his own screen. At last, Michelle's response appeared.

I'm not sure he knows enough computer stuff to worry about how much computer stuff I know.

I love it when you talk nerdy to me, Kayla teased.

Michelle didn't miss a beat. I could tell you how to rig a thingamajig with a doohickey, but then I'd lose my mystique. What are you and Sergeant Smokin' Hot up to today?

Kayla tried to tell herself the glance in Ryan's direction was reflex, but she never could master self-deception. Rather than attempting to fool her friend, she tried for something breezy and casual with a side of snark.

Settling in at our new nest. Making a shared shopping list. Global thermonuclear war. Trying not to think about the killer on the loose. You know, the usual, she responded, hoping a dose of flippancy would be enough to mask exactly how uncomfortable she was with this entire "personal-protection" situation.

Always the same old...

How's my law firm?

Still standing. There was a pause and the ellipses disappeared. She was about to set aside the phone when the dots popped up again. My friend at the Bureau is telling me Del signed in from another IP address today. He's been on the move lately.

Kayla pursed her lips, doing her best to ignore the creeping feeling that was crawling up the back of her neck. As far as she knew, Ty's nephew was a homebody, of sorts. He wasn't a social creature, like his cousin Trey had been. He didn't party, like Trey and the other young attorneys at the firm did. He was quiet. Happy to fade into the background. More difficult to know, and therefore to read. All things she'd once considered attributes. Now, his habits—or lack of them—came across as something more menacing.

He is a homebody. The fact he's moving around is making me nervous, she admitted, finding it easier to be open via text than talking.

I hear you. But at the moment, the more important thing is to be sure you aren't a sitting duck.

You've been spending too much time with Lieutenant Looker.

You should have heard my snort, Michelle responded. I'll be using your pet name for him later.

TMI.

Kayla must have cringed as she typed out the letters, because Ryan's gruff inquiry startled her so much the phone almost squirted out of her hand.

"What's wrong?"

"Oh. Nothing," she said, reflexively closing her phone screen when she looked up and found him watching her.

"You had a look on your face just now," he insisted, gesturing to his own face.

"I was… My friend was making a bad joke."

"Okay." He resumed typing. Without looking up, he asked, "Any sign of Del Powers?"

"He isn't coming into the office," she reported.

Her brow furrowed when she realized he hadn't asked if the friend she referred to was Michelle. "Hey, how did you know I was texting Michelle?"

"Hmm?" He looked up at last, his forehead furrowed.

"How did you know it was Michelle I was texting?" she repeated, waggling her phone at him.

His eyebrows shot up, and a slow, sheepish smile tugged at the corner of his mouth. Ryan set his phone on the counter as hers vibrated with an alert. "It's my job to pay attention to you." He hesitated for a moment. "I'm not trying to invade your privacy, it's—"

His explanation was cut off by his own phone. Kayla saw Ethan Scott's name flash on the screen before Ryan swiped it away to accept the call. "Hey. Got anything?"

She glanced down at the notification on her own screen. Apparently, he was done updating their combined shopping list. Her thumb hovered over the icon to open the app even as she chastised herself for being too curious to see what he'd added. But then Ryan gave a low grunt. She glanced up to see him scowling fiercely as he listened to whatever Ethan was relaying on the other end.

"What? What is it?" she asked in an urgent whisper.

He gave his head a slight shake, then signaled he was still getting information. At last, his scowl faded into a grim line as he nodded. "Okay. We'll hang tight," he said into the phone. "Check in with you later."

"What? What happened?" she demanded as he ended the call.

"Nothing happened," he assured her. "But it looks like we need to pare the list down to where we can stay nimble and be ready to move," he said, regret tingeing his tone.

"Why? How can anyone possibly know where we are?"

He nodded to her phone. "Maybe he's more tech-savvy than we thought." Sighing, he ran a hand over his face. "Anyway, he hasn't been returning calls from the police, so Ethan finally got the search warrant for Del's place."

"Did they find anything?"

Ryan shook his head, his expression grave. "More about what they didn't find. His work clothes and car are still there. The cleaner he had coming in weekly showed up at near the same time Ethan and his team did. She said the place looked like he hadn't slept there for a couple of days or more, but he hadn't informed the cleaning service he'd be going out of town, which was unusual for him."

"I can't even begin to guess what is usual for Del,"

she murmured. "He's definitely not the guy I thought I knew." The wound in her arm ached. She reached up to cover it with her hand, hoping the pressure would ease the pain away. "But he didn't pack anything?"

"He didn't pack any suits," Ryan corrected. "According to the cleaning woman, nothing appeared to be missing except the outdoors gear he kept in the garage. Said he had a whole other wardrobe in a cabinet out there. Didn't like his suits smelling like fish, I guess."

"I take it the cabinet was empty."

"Yes." He drummed his fingers on the countertop. "He also took a kayak, his fishing gear and left the gun safe unlocked."

"And empty," she concluded.

"Yes."

"And they think it all means…" She trailed off meaningfully.

"We think it means Del Powers has gone to ground."

Chapter Five

"Again, I've gotta say I think this is a bad idea," Ryan grumbled as he followed her through the front door of Powers, Powers & Walton the following morning.

"Your objections have been noted for the record, but overruled," Kayla replied without glancing back at him. As she made a beeline for the midcentury command console helmed by a young blonde receptionist, Kayla searched her memory for the young woman's name. Brittney? Brianna?

"Mrs. Powers." The receptionist blurted her name in a half-shout as she shot to her feet, her headset hooked over one ear. "You're here."

"I'm here. How are you… Bailey?" The name came to her in a flash of pain-laced memory. Tyrone had once joked the young woman was so effusive, he wouldn't dare offer her a cup of coffee much less the Irish coffee better suited to her name. It was one of those silly things he liked to say. A prototypically groan-worthy dad joke, and Kayla had loved laughing at them with him.

"I'm fine, ma'am." The younger woman tilted her

head. "I didn't expect… I mean… It's nice to see you," she said at last.

"Thank you." She offered her warmest smile.

"We didn't expect you to come in today."

She glanced over at Ryan Hastings, who was taking in every inch of the reception-area decor. He couldn't have looked more like a cop if she had dressed him in uniform and handed him a baton. "This is Sergeant Hastings from the Arkansas State Police," she said, seeing no point in concealing her companion's identity. "I stopped by to speak to Ms. Fraser."

"Ms. Fraser is in her office. Would you like me to buzz up there?"

Kayla shook her head. "Don't bother. If she's busy I'll wait," she answered breezily. "Come in, Sergeant, I'll show you around. Play your cards right and I'll let you score a cup of coffee from the world's fanciest coffee machine," she said as she blew past the reception desk, her gaze set on the open-riser staircase leading to the firm's upper floor.

"I don't need any coffee," Ryan grumbled as he lengthened his strides to catch up with her. "Isn't there a back door we could've come in through?"

Kayla hiked her handbag into the crook of her arm, tilted up her chin and sent him a quelling look. "This is my firm. I'm not coming in through the back door."

"You realize this defeats the whole keeping-a-low-profile plan," he huffed as they made their way up the stairs.

Kayla kept her gaze fixed straight ahead, all too aware of the murmurs and stares coming from the attorneys and assistants who worked in the bullpen on the first floor. "It's important for them to see me," she said softly. "It's important for everyone to see me."

She switched her handbag to her right arm as they turned the corner on the landing. Her left still ached like the devil, but she was loathe to show any weakness in front of Ryan. He'd add her injury to his long list of reasons why she shouldn't do whatever she wanted to do.

"Listen, I understand you think it's important to put face time in the office," he said . "But surely you know somebody here is likely in touch with Del Powers or his father. Somebody is going to let them know you came in today."

As Kayla reached the top of the stairs, she stopped and turned to face him. "I'm counting on it."

"This is a dangerous game," he warned, pitching his voice low.

"It's not a game, it's my life. I'll play it safe as much as I can, but I'm not about to let someone else dictate how I live it." She leaned in, holding his gaze steady. "I make the rules."

He nodded, then twisted to look around. "Give me the lay of the land." He gestured to the closed doors surrounding them. "Looks like no one is here."

"This is the executive level. Michelle is working out of Tyrone's old office these days." She gestured toward one of the doors leading into a corner office. She shuddered when she thought of Michelle's old office on the first floor and the frosted pane of glass shattered into a million tiny pieces by a bullet fired by an unknown intruder. "The one she was using downstairs needed some repairs."

Someone took a shot at her friend. Had it been Del?

A shiver raced down her spine. Shaking it off, she pointed to the opposite corner. "Bill's office. Senator Powers," she corrected. "Obviously, he's not practicing law here, but Tyrone wanted to keep it for him to use when he came to town."

"Does he?" Ryan asked, quirking an eyebrow.

"He used to," she replied. "Like Del, I don't think he's been here since the will was probated."

Ryan pressed his lips together, nodding as he digested the information. "Are they contesting it?"

"They've made threats, but as of yet, I don't believe anything has been filed."

"They won't."

Startled by the confidence in his assertion, she glanced over at him. "What makes you so sure?"

"If they were serious about wanting the place, they'd have started the process. Plus, if they wanted the firm so badly, Del Powers would be here all day, every day, hanging on to the place even if his father can't."

She frowned as she parsed through his logic. "They said they wouldn't come in as long as I was in charge."

"And if they had a legal way of removing you as the boss, no one would need to take shots at you when you go out for a walk."

Pivoting, she met his gaze directly, resisting the urge to cover her aching bicep with a protective hand. "You think Del was trying to shoot to kill?"

To her relief, he gave a quick shake of his head. "I think he was shooting to scare. But I also think they won't hesitate to raise the stakes. They have a lot on the line, and you're an obstacle no one banked on needing to hurdle."

"Sergeant, I'm not an obstacle, I'm an immovable object," she replied tartly.

She turned on her heel, leaving the truth bomb she dropped in her wake. *Immovable* was her new keyword. Ryan had given her a half-dozen good reasons not to come into the office, and she'd ignored every one of them. She spotted people darting away from the bottom of the staircase when she turned and had little doubt they were hurrying to spread the word of her arrival.

This visit would be nothing more than a flyby. A bit of showboating to let them know she wasn't scared. Or, at least, to make them think she wasn't. Truthfully, Del's disappearance left her more unsettled than she wanted to admit.

The man she knew was a creature of habit. A person who liked numbers, order and routine. The idea of him deviating from the image she had of him in her mind was disconcerting. Of all the people in the Powers sphere of influence, Del was the last she would have expected to go rogue.

She caught the sound of Ryan Hastings's heavy footfalls right behind her and forced herself to breathe evenly. The last time she'd been in this office, the gun someone had used to murder her husband had fallen out of Tyrone's wall safe and landed with its muzzle pointed directly at her.

She wasn't ready to do more than make an appearance, but by the same token, she wasn't ready to concede this space to William and Del Powers's acolytes. Tyrone had left the firm in her care, and he had compelling reasons for his decision.

Ryan must have sensed her faltering. "Are you okay?" he asked, his voice quiet and compelling.

"I'm fine. This won't take long," she assured him.

Her steps slowed when she saw Tyrone's longtime assistant, Nancy Ayers, rising from her desk, a look of concerned confusion furrowing her forehead.

"What are you doing here?" the older woman blurted. Then, as if the impertinent question was a starter's pistol, she shot out from behind her desk. "I mean to say, Ms. Fraser had me thinking you wouldn't be coming back to the office for some time now."

"I'm only here for a moment," Kayla replied, wincing only a little as Nancy pulled her into a hard, fast hug.

"Well, you know we're keeping everything running as tight as we can around here," Nancy assured her. "You take all the time you need, bless your heart."

Kayla straightened with a smile, wondering exactly which variation of the multipurpose Southernism Ty's secretary was employing. Pity? Sympathy? Annoyance? Or was it honeyed condescension?

"Is she busy? With someone?"

"Lieutenant Scott came in earlier, but I think she's reviewing case files at the moment." She made a show of peering over Kayla's shoulder at Ryan. "Do you want me to buzz her and tell her you and your, uh, friend are here?"

Kayla smiled. Nancy Ayers was *über*competent in all fields except subtlety. "Nancy, this is Sergeant Hastings from the Arkansas State Police. He works with Lieutenant Scott," she added with a cordial nod. "Sergeant Hastings, this is Nancy Ayers, the woman who truly runs P, P and W."

Nancy ducked her head but didn't bother trying to deny the assertion. "I see. Nice to meet you."

"It's a pleasure, ma'am," Ryan said, extending his hand.

Nancy took it, her warm smile unfurling at the polite greeting. "Call me Nancy, please."

Ready to continue her mission, Kayla gestured toward the door to Ty's old office. "No need to buzz, I'll give her a knock before I burst in."

The office door swung inward, and Michelle stood framed in the opening. "No need. Someone forgot to remove me from the office early warning system when I moved up here." She stared hard at Nancy. "And don't you tip them off. I like knowing my presence instills unrest."

Kayla rolled her eyes and started toward her friend. "The FBI should have given you the title 'Special Agent of Chaos' when they planted you here." She waved Ryan in the direction of the office. "This will only take a minute."

"Early warning system?" he asked Michelle as she stepped aside to allow them to pass.

"A group text the associates use to alert one another one of the partners is on site," she explained, closing the door behind them. The minute the latch clicked, she turned on Kayla. "Is this your idea of keeping a low profile? If so, you're bad at it."

"Maybe, but I'm awesome at playing Whac-A-Mole," Kayla said, dropping her handbag into one of the guest chairs.

"Is this what this is?" Ryan asked, his back pressed against the closed door. "Are you popping your head out?"

"Perhaps a bit," she admitted.

"What's going on?" Michelle asked, her innate lawyer's caution creeping through in her tone.

"Ryan didn't want me to come into the office, but I thought it was important to show my face," Kayla explained.

"Okay, so you agreed to disagree," Michelle responded with a diplomatic nod. "What prompted this unexpected, yet delightful, drop-in? It wouldn't have anything to do with Del Powers going on an unannounced vacation, would it?"

Ryan shrugged. "Mrs. Powers thought it was important to be seen in the office."

As if on cue, Michelle's phone dinged. She glanced over at the device lying on its charging station. "I'm betting confirmation of the sighting has hit the wires."

"See?" Pleased with herself, Kayla plucked her handbag from the chair and looped it over her arm as she cast a pointed glance in Ryan's direction. "I told you we wouldn't be here long."

"And I told you it wasn't a good idea to come anywhere near this place. How do you know we won't be followed when we leave?"

"Oh, but I'm hoping we are. We're making a public exit right now," she announced. She crossed to her friend and gave Michelle a one-armed squeeze. "You should be able to access the lobby camera on Tyrone's desktop," she murmured.

"I'm already binge-watching the show," Michelle assured her. "Go. Get out of here, you troublemaker. I'll call you later."

"Talk to you later," Kayla confirmed, then headed

straight to the door. Ryan stood in her path, tall and unmoving. "Come on, Sergeant, we need to get a move on if we're going to get any snitches to scurry."

He blinked as if needing a moment to process her meaning, then grasped the door handle and pulled it open. "After you, ma'am."

"Don't *ma'am* me," she murmured as she swept past him.

She could hear the smile in his voice without turning to look back at him.

Kayla made a beeline for the stairs, blowing kisses at Nancy Ayers and quelling the older woman's sputters of protest with promises to call her soon. Her heels clattered on the steps, alerting everyone below of her imminent arrival.

By the time they reached the bottom, most of the employees in the warren of cubicles had their heads down and their fingers moving furiously across keyboards. She wondered how much gibberish was being generated for show. Still, she didn't break stride as she lifted a hand to wave to the few brave souls who looked up from their pseudo work.

By the time they hit reception, Bailey was seated at her desk with her hands folded neatly on the work surface and her eyes fixed on the doorway.

The girl jumped when they blew past her. "Mrs. Powers," she chirped. "Are you leaving already?"

"Yes. I only needed to pass something along to Michelle," Kayla said briskly.

"Nice to see you again," Bailey called as Kayla marched through to the vestibule.

Ryan nodded an acknowledgment as Kayla held

the door open for him. He shot her a stern glare as he passed, then pushed open the outer door. He made a point of checking the foot traffic in both directions before allowing her out into the glaring afternoon sunlight.

Within minutes, they were ensconced in his bland, state-issued SUV, and headed away from downtown Bentonville.

"I'm still not exactly sure what you are hoping to gain," he said after three minutes of tense silence passed between them.

Kayla sighed heavily, then pulled her phone from her bag. When he slowed to a stop at an intersection, she held it up to show him the screen filling with message bubbles from Michelle.

"I gained the names of two people who left the office hot on our heels."

He cast her a sidelong glance as the light turned green and he accelerated. "What do you think that proves?"

"I'm pretty sure it's going to lead to someone alerting Del to our presence."

"I thought you said he wasn't one to hang out with the office crowd," he reminded her.

"He wasn't. At least, not to my knowledge. But that didn't mean he was a loner. He had friends. Or at least people who would act like friends to get close to a senator's son."

"And the names are?"

"Chet Barrow and Joshua Potter."

"Who are they?" Ryan prompted.

"Two of Trey Powers's closest friends. They were on Trey's boat the night Mallory Murray went missing."

"I thought you said Trey and Del didn't socialize with one another outside of family functions. He wasn't out on the boat with them, was he?"

"No, but Trey is gone now, and you know how nature abhors a vacuum," she said with an airy wave of her hand. "With me out of the office, Del would be the most likely candidate for these two sycophants to suck up to, wouldn't he?"

He made a grunting sound she assumed to be agreement. "I'm assuming Michelle has already fed information to Ethan Scott?" he asked without inflection.

"No doubt," Kayla answered.

She dropped her phone back into her bag and let her head fall against the seat rest, sighing as she rolled her neck back and forth. She stopped when she was facing him. "I know you didn't like this plan, but we can't sit in some hidey-hole and do nothing. Listen, you gave me this, so I'll promise to lay low for a few days. Deal?"

"Is this how it's going to be? Are we bartering for your safety?"

"No, but I'm also not going to be stashed away because it's the easier option. At some point this has to come to an end. I need it to happen sooner rather than later."

He draped a hand over the top of the steering wheel and glanced over at her. "Listen, I understand you're under a lot of pressure, and you're eager to get your life back on track, but you can't put a timeline on these things. Sometimes they have to run their natural course."

Kayla sighed, closed her eyes for a moment, then

whispered, "I have to put a time line on it. I need this to be over once and for all."

"I understand—"

"No, you don't understand anything," she said, interrupting him before he could feed her another line of platitudes. After drawing a deep breath, she let the truth go on an explosive exhale. "I have to know it's safe for me to bring Ty's baby into this world, and I can't do that if the people responsible for his death are the ones making the rules."

Ryan's head whipped around, and he hooked a sharp right into the driveway of a semi-occupied strip mall. Instinctively, Kayla reached for the handle above the door to brace herself. When the SUV jerked to a stop with a sharp squeal of brakes, she stared back at his shocked expression impassively.

"You're pregnant?" he asked, incredulous.

Kayla's answering smile was small, but genuine in its pleasure. She nodded, blinking back tears as she tried not to imagine all the ways she might have broken the happy news to Tyrone himself.

"Surprise," she whispered, then pressed a knuckle to her lips in time to suppress a hiccup of a sob.

Chapter Six

He'd done his best not to pry after she dropped her pregnancy bombshell on him, and she hadn't offered anything but the barest facts. She was pregnant, Tyrone Powers was the father and no one else knew. Not even Michelle and Ethan. And she didn't want them to know yet.

The last part bothered him the most. Why had she told him when she hadn't even told her friends? But it didn't take long for him to work out the reason why. The child she was carrying would be Tyrone's heir. A fact that made her even more of a target.

Kayla was true to her word. After their brief appearance at PP&W, she'd stuck to the rental house in Fayetteville. As far as Ryan could tell, she spent her days reading, attending to bits of firm business Michelle sent over and avoiding him. Other than conversations about grocery lists or food-delivery orders, they'd hardly done more than exchange polite pleasantries for three days.

Now they were moving locations.

She'd been quiet as she watched the scenery around them change from strip malls to subdivisions to sprawling suburban spreads. He chanced a glance at her as he turned onto the county highway that would take them to their next location, and saw the slight lift of one pale eyebrow.

But still, she said nothing.

Unable to contain himself any longer, Ryan broke the silence. "I got us a cabin."

She turned to look at him, and he saw both eyebrows lift a millimeter more. "A cabin?"

"A nice one," he quickly added, but immediately regretted it. This woman was accustomed to luxury homes. A cabin rated exceptional on the Staycation site might look nice to him, but it would more likely resemble a hovel to her. "Well, you know. Clean. Comfortable."

She pursed her lips, but he was fairly sure he caught the beginnings of smile before he turned his attention back to the road.

"Clean and comfortable are nice," she said in a tone of exaggerated encouragement.

He chuckled. "Well, it's on Beaver Lake, so maybe that will add to the appeal."

Apparently, he'd said the magic words, because Kayla sat up, angling to look at him. "You rented a cabin on Beaver Lake?"

"I thought it would be good to get out of town, and you said you liked staying at your place on the lake..." He trailed off, wishing he hadn't even hinted at a comparison between the cabin he'd booked online and the massive castle on Table Rock Lake she'd inherited from her late husband. "I thought the water would be nice," he finished sheepishly.

"It will," she reassured him with gratifying speed.

"I could only get it for two nights, so it won't be long." Ryan wondered if he was trying to reassure her or temper expectations.

"That's fine."

"And, you know, it's not one of those luxury cabins—"

"I told you I didn't grow up with money. Why do you keep acting like I'm some pampered princess who's going to throw a fit if my sheets aren't silk?"

The image of Kayla Powers's blonde wavy hair trailing across a slinky white pillowcase flared in his mind, but he quickly squelched it.

Heat crept up his neck and set the tips of his ears on fire. Inwardly, he cursed his ancestors for blessing him with his red hair and the complexion that went with it. Groping for something to say, he fell back on offense as the best defense for his wayward thoughts.

"Bet it didn't take you long to get used to it," he muttered. He could feel her gaze on his profile, but he didn't dare look at her.

"Some parts of it were easier than others," she said at last.

Grateful for the conversational gambit she lobbed his way, he dove in. "I can take a guess at which parts were easier, but what was harder for you?" he asked, genuinely curious.

She was quiet so long he was afraid she wouldn't answer, but at last she spoke. "Most people think getting rich is the hard part. They don't realize all the work that goes into staying rich."

He chanced a peek at her. "How do you mean?"

She shrugged. "Most of those people are born with some sort of cushion. I had your average middle-class childhood, but even the poorest of Ty's friends would have thought my parents were paupers."

"I see," he conceded as he signaled a right turn.

"I don't think you can," she said dryly. "There are strata within the social stratum. Layers as thin and transparent as puff pastry, but as strong and pungent as an onion."

"Way to nail those analogies," he said, matching her tone. "But I do have some clue. My mother's husband has money."

She turned in her seat again, her interest piqued. "Your stepfather?"

He gave her a lopsided smirk. "He was no more my stepfather than Trey Powers your stepson."

Kayla inclined her head. "Point taken."

"Anyhow, back to what was harder," he reminded her.

She chuckled. "You're a dogged one, aren't you?"

"I'm curious. You went to Yale Law, so you had to have some clue what it was like to move among the moneyed."

"Yeah, I did." She paused as if needing time for reflection. "I guess the hardest part to master was taking it all as seriously as they do. You'd think with all that money and all that power, people would be satisfied, but they never are, are they?"

He shook his head, but kept his mouth shut, wanting to hear her take on the phenomenon.

"Even Ty. As comfortable as he was with his life, he hated the thought of someone having more influence or control than he did. His need to be the master of his universe was what drove him to suspect Harold Dennis was making some kind of move."

"Oh?" He tapped the brakes to slow the car as the pavement gave way to a gravel road, but hoped she'd keep talking.

"Of course, he would have said he was protecting the firm from any possible repercussions if one of Hal's shady real-estate deals went south, but honestly? I think he was more afraid one of them would succeed spectacularly. Hal may have been his mentor in many ways, but he was still Ty's father's hired hand."

"Do you think your husband was playing both ends against the middle?"

She stared straight through the windshield, not even sparing him a glance when she answered. "I think my husband was doing what he was raised to do—protect the status quo."

"And you had a hard time doing the same?"

"Let's say I needed some training wheels when it came to walking the party line."

Ryan had to tamp down a surge of guilt. He'd always thought his mother was being weak when she went along with her new husband's wishes. He never considered the possibility she was feeling her way through her new life. A typical teenager, he was more focused on how the change in her relationship status impacted him, not how hard it had to be for her.

"Must have been difficult," he said, trying to keep his tone neutral.

Kayla sighed. "Some of it was tricky. The keeping up with who had what and trying to make sure people thought we were more than one step ahead of them." She paused and drummed her fingertips on her leg. "Hard to pretend you care about the approval of people who clearly don't care about you as a person." He glanced over and she wrinkled her nose. "I probably didn't make any sense there."

"It made perfect sense," he assured her as the rutted road opened into a clearing and the modern log cabin came into view. A slice of the blue lake sparkled beyond the wraparound porch.

"Oh."

He wasn't sure how to read Kayla's soft exhale. Was it one of surprised delight or dread? "Is that a good *oh*, or a bad one?"

"Good," she said, a self-conscious laugh burbling from her. "Definitely good. This looks lovely. Being on the water always relaxes me."

"Alright, then. I'm glad." Gravel crunched under the tires as he slowed to a halt. "I brought most of the stuff we had at the house and replenished the perishables," he informed her as they opened the car doors.

She walked to the corner of the porch and stopped, peering around the house at the lake as if she was using the cabin as cover. Concerned, Ryan opened the liftgate, but abandoned the contents of the SUV in favor of finding out what was eating at his client.

"What's wrong?" he asked, drawing to a halt about a foot behind her and scanning the area for possible threats.

Kayla hugged herself tightly for a moment, then blew out a breath as she let her arms fall, her shoulder visibly dropping. "Absolutely nothing." This time, she gave him a smile that reached up and lit her eyes. "I'm happy to have the lake view, even if it is only for a couple of days."

"I'll keep that in mind. In the meantime, we should get our stuff and get inside," he said gruffly.

"Hopefully, you won't have to search out too many lake properties for me." Kayla brushed past him on the way back to the SUV. "But I guess I'm going to have to learn to pack lighter if we're going to keep moving so often," she commented as she pulled a designer suitcase she'd stowed in the back of the vehicle. She set it on the ground at her feet with a huff then blew her hair out of her face.

"If I offer to carry your bag for you, am I being helpful or sexist?" he asked with a tight half-smile.

"Depends on whether or not you believe I can handle my own suitcase," she replied.

"I'm prepared to believe you can handle anything life throws at you." He glanced and pointed at her left arm, then met her gaze again. "I know it's healing, but it still has to hurt to strain your muscles."

"I'm secure enough in my power to allow you to carry my bag, as long as you understand my muscles are unquestionably up to the task," she drawled.

"I have no doubt," he said as he lifted the heavy suitcase with ease then grabbed his own nylon duffel from the cargo hold and swung the strap over his shoulder. "Go on ahead," he urged her. "The code for the door lock is three-seven-nine-one," he told her.

She started up the path toward the front door. "You've already memorized it?"

"The owner used the last four of my phone number," he explained. "I hate it when they do that. Don't they know how vulnerable it makes both their tenants and the properties?"

"I'm sure you'll point it out to them in your review." Kayla reached the front door, punched in the code and swung the glass pane door inward. "Cozy."

It was a nice cabin. Possibly the nicest cabin he'd ever seen—and growing up in Arkansas, he'd seen quite a few. Once over the threshold, the rustic exterior gave way to a modern, comfortable interior with an open-concept floor plan and towering ceilings. He noted a ladder to a sleeping loft to his left, but rolled her suitcase into one of the two bedrooms off the hallway leading from the living area. Once again, he left her belongings in the main room with its en suite bathroom, then dropped his own duffel in the room opposite. When he turned, he found Kayla standing in the short hall glancing from her room to his, her bottom lip caught between her teeth.

"If you want, I can sleep up in the loft, but I'd prefer not to," he said with a grimace. "I'm not sure how my knee will do with the ladder."

Kayla waved off the suggestion and then gave a sharp shake of her head. "Don't be silly. There's plenty of room for both of us." She turned around to face the open living area again, with its wide wall of windows that showcased the shimmering lake.

"This is beautiful," she said quietly.

"Not as impressive as your house on Table Rock, but, yes, this is nice."

Kayla rolled her eyes then strolled into the living room, trailing her fingers over the fabrics of the sofa cushions and throws artfully tossed over stuffed armchairs that faced a stone fireplace. "You mean not as obnoxious as the house on Table Rock." When he said nothing, she gave a short laugh. "Don't worry, I am aware the house is both ostentatious and beautiful," she said with a twinkle in her eye. "I have an attachment to it, but I can admit it isn't exactly to my taste."

"I would think a place so impressive would be to anybody's taste."

"Don't get me wrong, I'm not complaining. It's simply not what I would have chosen for a lake house. Too over-the-top. Then again, I'm told Ty's father had a massive ego, so the size and style of the house probably suited him."

This place suited her. The thought popped into his head unbidden, but true. The decor was soft and welcoming. Bright and airy, but still plush. Almost sumptuous.

Needing to rein in his thoughts before his assessment got out of hand, Ryan pointed to the front door. "I'm gonna go grab the groceries. I'll be right back." He strode out the door, making a beeline for the SUV.

He didn't need to be having thoughts about how perfect she'd looked in the comfortably luxurious cabin he'd chosen. Didn't want to think too hard about how it pleased him to please her. If he stayed in the house with her, soon his brain would be waxing poetics about the way her face lit every time she turned her gaze toward the water. And distracted thinking like that got people hurt.

Leaning into the cargo area, he snagged the handles of multiple grocery bags and hefted them with a grunt. He turned and straightened abruptly when he nearly stepped on Kayla's foot. "Ow!" he howled when he hit his head on the open liftgate. "Ugh."

"Sorry. I thought you knew I'd be right behind you," she said in a rush. "Here, let me carry some of those."

He surrendered the bags from his left hand and automatically reached up to rub the soreness from his scalp. "I can get the rest."

"I'm not helpless, and you're not here to fetch and carry for me," she countered, turning on her heel.

He huffed as he reached into the SUV to get the remainder of the groceries. When they had everything inside, he locked the door and put the chain on out of habit. He turned to find her watching him, her expression dark.

"What?"

"Did you bring me to the lake to lock me in?"

"Huh? Oh!" He glanced back at the door and felt his ears heat with a blush. "No. Sorry, I... Habit."

She tipped her head to the side as she unloaded one of the shopping bags. "Occupational hazard?"

"Occupational safeguard," he corrected.

They worked together swiftly and efficiently, and in a matter of minutes, they had their provisions stored. When the last bag was stowed under the sink, Kayla turned to him, her expression open and hopeful. "Can I go down to the lake?"

He nodded. "Of course, we can."

"You'll come, too?"

"I will need to stay reasonably nearby, but I'll do my best to give you whatever space you need," he assured her.

To his surprise, Kayla shook her head adamantly. "Not what I meant. I...I want to go down to the dock. Do you want to come, too?"

"Sure. Let's go check it out," he replied.

He saw no reason to tell her he'd already been out to the property to inspect the area. The floating slip was tucked in a small cove, but was bracketed by docks belonging to the neighbors on either side. The area at the front of the cabin was wooded, but the shoreline had been cleared and tamed. A few oaks and maples provided shade, but the rest was the work of a landscaper rather than Mother Nature.

He followed Kayla down the flagstone steps that led to a small dock. He wasn't about to miss this opportunity to get her to talk more. Choosing a lakefront property had been a good idea. She was more relaxed here than she'd been in the tidy house in the nondescript subdivision.

She might not be completely on board with the plan for her protection, but whether she realized it or not, Kayla was beginning to open up.

Not that he was going to point it out. She said being on the water relaxed her. Perhaps he could get her to talk some about her pregnancy.

He understood the need for secrecy. The birth of this child would certainly not be cause for celebration for the remainder of the Powers family. But was she happy about it? Was she excited to have a child by the man she clearly had loved, or would the baby be a painful reminder of all she'd lost?

Regardless, this pregnancy put her in even more danger than anyone anticipated, and he was going to do his best to protect her and her child.

She walked out to the end of the dock and kicked off her sandals before sitting down on the edge of the weather-resistant resin planks. Though the seasons were turning, the afternoon sun was warm. The sky was bright blue and cloudless. Kayla tipped up her chin to the bright rays. With her eyes shut, she spoke softly. "I have to tell you something."

"What?" he asked, instantly on high alert.

"I had a text from Bill Powers this morning."

He tensed, but kept his mouth shut. Now he had an explanation for why she hadn't resisted the move. But it ticked him off she'd held on to this information for more than two minutes. Worse, he could tell by her glance she knew it would make him worry and did it, anyway. He bit his tongue, refusing to rise to the bait.

"Your basic, how-are-you-doing, we're-all-thinking-about-you text," she said, pulling her phone from the front pocket of her jeans.

He remained stubbornly silent while she unlocked the device and opened the message, holding it out for him to see.

Hope U got the rest you needed at Briarwood. Hope 2 have this mess with Ty's estate straightened out asap. Plz call.

While he frowned at the message, Kayla peered over his arm. "I always find it weird when people use text abbreviations, but throw in all the appropriate punctuation. I mean, are you being lazy or not?"

His eyebrows jumped at the snide edge in her tone, but he let it go. "Did you call him?"

She scoffed. "Of course not."

"Did you tell them you were going to Briarwood?"

"No."

"Probably not hard for them to figure it out, though. Do they know what you were being treated for?"

"Michelle and I figured we'd go with grief, exhaustion and general depression if anyone dared to ask."

"Did they try to contact you while you were at the facility?"

"I didn't have my phone for the time I was in treatment, but Bill did try to talk to Michelle while I was there."

"What can you tell me about his relationship with his son?"

Kayla eyed him as if it was a trick question. "There are worse relationships," she said cautiously. "Del was his son from his first marriage. It's my understanding Bill's divorce from his ex-wife was contentious. He remarried and had two more children with his current wife. Del's mother passed away before he went off to college. Ty said their relationship improved after she was gone."

"Would you say they are close?" Ryan probed.

She paused as if selecting each word carefully. "I would say Del would like to secure his place in his father's world."

Kayla met his gaze directly, so he asked a direct question. "Do you think in his mind that entails clearing the way for his father's ambitions?"

Kayla shrugged. "I don't know. Truthfully, I didn't know either of them well enough to have any depth of knowledge concerning their motivations. Mostly I saw superficial stuff. In public, the Powers family always presented a united front."

"Do you think it's possible Del is in contact with his father now?"

"Possible?" She raised an eyebrow. "Of course. But I don't believe he is acting with his father's blessing, if you're thinking Bill was part of it."

"What makes you say so?"

"Tyrone and Bill were brothers. They were close when they were younger. Trey was his nephew. He may have grown up to be a spoiled jerk, but I assume he was once a cute kid like any other. Aside from any familial affection, Bill is a politician. It's his nature to avoid anything that might blow back on him. He has presidential ambitions. He's not going to do anything that could cause long-term damage to his reputation."

"A son who may or may not be a loose cannon can be an enormous liability."

"Del is not the son Bill trots out into the spotlight," she reminded him, her voice soft. "If there's anything the Powers men excel at, it's controlling the optics of the situation. Tyrone was no different."

Ryan was surprised by the implied criticism of her late husband. He wanted to believe a tragic death meant a person should be canonized a saint, but he was thrown off by Kayla's offhanded acknowledgment of her husband's flaws. Undoubtedly, her stay at Briarwood had included at least a session or two of grief counselling. And her training as an attorney had taught her not to volunteer information unless asked a direct question.

Keeping that in mind, he charged straight into the topic.

"We haven't talked about your pregnancy—"

"I'm not ready to," she said without a beat of hesitation.

"But you told me—" he began, hoping to draw at least a little more information from her before she froze him out again.

"Because knowing I am pregnant is germane to your mission here," she replied. "My feelings on my pregnancy are not."

He was still formulating his rebuttal to this logic when the crack of a gunshot echoed across the lake. Ryan's arm shot out, and they hit the water with a splash.

Chapter Seven

Water went straight up her nose. She swallowed a good gulp of it, too. Thankfully, she'd been taking a breath in preparation for putting Sergeant Hastings in his place with regard to her personal life when he'd toppled them both into the surprisingly chilly water. He held her tight against his torso, his arm a steel band around her waist as he propelled them to the surface.

Kayla burst from the water, sputtering and gasping. "What—" He tightened his grip on her and tugged, using one arm to push them back until they were both sheltered beneath the dock.

"Gunshots," he whispered in a low urgent voice. "Shout at me later. Voices carry across the water."

She opened then shut her mouth again, gazing at him in disbelief. Then a volley of gunshots rang out across the water of the lake.

"Oh, my God." Wriggling in his grasp, she turned to look him straight in the eye. "Those *are* gunshots," she whispered, her eyes wide.

He braced one hand against the underside of the dock, but did not ease his hold on her. He tilted his head to one side, clearly listening for more. Her own breathing sounded like a rush of wind in the silence between them.

She picked up the distant hum of a boat motor. Water slapped against the dock's pilings. Birdsong. Birds tweeted and trilled all around them. How could birds be singing when someone was shooting at her again?

Sure enough, another barrage of gunfire jolted her from her reverie. Kayla went stiff against Ryan's chest, her hands digging into his broad shoulders as she anchored herself to him.

"Six rounds," he whispered to her. "I don't think someone is shooting at us, but I can't get a good bead on which direction it's coming from. Water messes with the sound."

To her horror, her teeth began to chatter. Ryan shifted slightly, bringing her chest flush against his.

"Hang in a couple minutes. I know you're already cold. We won't stay in here too long."

He pushed off the underside of the dock, moving them closer to the ladder attached to the side, but keeping them sheltered beneath it.

"I'm going up to make sure the area is clear." He physically removed one of her hands from where she'd embedded it on his shoulder and wrapped her chilled fingers around the handle of the ladder. "Stay right here. I'll let you know when it's okay to come up."

Kayla nodded mutely as she watched him clamber up the ladder, water sluicing from his sodden clothes. Squeezing her eyes shut, she listened to his heavy footballs as he strode the length of the dock. He stopped the moment the report of a bullet being fired split the air. Five more shots followed in rapid succession. Clamping her chattering teeth together, she gripped the sides of the ladder with both hands and hauled herself up a few inches so the top of her head brushed the bottom of the dock. She felt trapped between the cold pull of the water and the echo of gunfire across its surface.

Ryan's footsteps shook the planks. The toes of his shoes appeared over the edge, water dripping down onto the top rung of the ladder.

"You can come up. It sounds like it's coming from the east. I'm pretty sure it's somebody out target shooting."

Kayla moved hand over hand to the outside of the ladder and planted her foot on the bottom rung to hoist herself out of the chilled water.

"Sometimes I hate living in a gun-happy state," she said through chattering teeth.

With her torso out of the water, Ryan offered both of his hands to help her up.

"It can feel like we're still living in the Wild West some days," he said dryly. "Come on, let's get inside and get changed. I think we're both going to need a hot shower."

Her sodden jeans and long-sleeve shirt clung to her as they made their way up the shore incline toward the cabin. They were approaching the sliding door when whoever was shooting let loose with another barrage.

Her back stiff, she walked past Ryan into the open kitchen she'd so admired a short time before—now, all she could see was how exposed the back half of the cabin was to anyone who was looking.

"D-Do you think we're o-okay here?" she stammered as she hugged herself tightly.

"Shower first. Get into some warm, dry clothes. We'll talk later," he said, planting his hand on the small of her back and propelling her toward the narrow hallway. "I'll make sure the house is secured and will wait to shower once you're finished."

"But you have to be freezing, too," she protested, glancing back over her shoulder.

"I'll grab a towel and dry off. It'll be okay," he said firmly.

As she stripped out of her cold, wet clothing, she couldn't help but wonder at the strange direction this new chapter of her life was taking.

Murder.

Mayhem.

She was being hunted by a man she thought she knew fairly well, but entrusting her life, and her most precious secrets, to a man she'd met barely a week ago.

Turning her face into the warm spray, she marveled at how quickly she'd grown accustomed to Ryan's quiet, competent company. She'd had no doubt he'd figure out where the shots were coming from and whether she was actually in danger. When he gave the all-clear, she didn't hesitate for a moment. Not even when second-guessing would be second nature to any rational human.

It was a novelty.

Before Tyrone, she'd only had one relationship that lasted beyond six months. All through college and law school, she'd kept her eyes fixed firmly on the future. Once she'd joined PP&W, she'd been buried too deep in the workload of an associate to find much time to socialize. Then she and Ty had hit it off, and before she knew it, they were married.

And though they'd lived together as husband and wife for a number of years, they'd never melded their lives. Ty was older, had an established group of friends whose wives were more his contemporaries than hers. And she couldn't hang around her former PP&W colleagues without draping whatever festivities they had planned with a giant wet blanket monogrammed with "the boss's wife."

She sighed as the hot water chased the cold from her bones, but she was all too aware of Ryan waiting for her to finish. After shutting off the water, she quickly dried off, then wrapped the towel snugly around her body.

As she pulled a pair of yoga pants and a sweatshirt from her suitcase, her mind whirred, trying to slot the events of the past week into some sort of order. But she couldn't. The past few months had been extraordinary, and not in the best way. As she pulled on the clothes, she considered talking to her counsellor about possible PTSD.

It was so odd to even consider talking to a stranger about such personal subjects. She'd grown up in a small town, where any gossip that even hinted at illness— physical or mental—carried the taint of stigma.

A thump from the other room jolted her from her ruminations. She pulled on her clothes, all the while thinking about how she could answer Ryan's questions about her pregnancy. She didn't know exactly how she felt beyond the most basic surges of happiness and fear. How was she supposed to express the jumble of emotions roiling inside her each time she let her mind wander in that direction?

She wasn't good at sharing. Ty had been one of the few people she'd let in. She'd thought she was a part of the Powers family, but Bill and Del were making it abundantly clear she'd been accepted only as a part of her husband's life, not on her own merit. Michelle and Ethan were the first people she'd taken into her confidence in years. And now, apparently, Ryan was a part of her circle. After all, she'd entrusted this near stranger with the most vital bit of information she'd ever shared with another living soul.

She opened the bedroom door and saw his door open at the opposite end of the hall. "I'm out of the shower. You can get in and get warm now."

Her heart rate shot up again when she caught a glimpse of Ryan as he exited his bedroom wearing nothing more than a towel wrapped around his waist. She blinked when it registered that the man had more than his fair share of muscles. She jumped when his deep voice came right back to her.

"Great. I'm getting in now. Do me a favor and stay in this part of the house? I don't want you to go near the windows until I've had a chance to give the area a more thorough check."

Backing away from her door, Kayla bumped up against the bed. Her knees bent automatically, and she dropped onto the firm mattress with her jaw agape.

"Kayla? Did you hear me?"

Was he coming this way? Dressed only in a towel?

"I heard you," she blurted as if the confirmation might ward him off. At the same time, her curiosity tugged her head to the side. Her cheeks flamed and she forced herself to straighten. She shouldn't be hoping for another glimpse of her protection agent in a towel.

She jumped up and paced the small area between the bed and the door. If she closed it now, would it be too obvious? Had he even noticed her door was open? She pressed the heel of her hand to the center of her forehead and forced herself to turn back to the suitcase she'd left open on the bed. The sound of water rushing through the pipes spurred her into action.

She'd unpack what she'd need for the next couple of days, then sort through the rest in an effort to pare down what she was carrying. Every place they were renting had laundry facilities, and it wasn't as if she needed an extensive wardrobe to hide out in Staycation homes. Her stubborn insistence on packing clothes she could wear into the office, or even out and about in Bentonville, now seemed as ridiculous to her as it must have been to Ryan. She'd sort it out and arrange for Michelle to collect the excess.

Ryan's shower took less than five minutes. She'd heard the water shut off, but stubbornly kept her back to the door. She didn't even allow herself to break from her task when she heard the click of his bedroom door. By the time she'd separated her clothing into piles of what to keep and what could go, she could hear him moving around the main room of the cabin.

She'd started to comb through her toiletries case when a soft beep indicated the disengagement of the lock. The cabin door opened and closed, and another beep assured her he'd secured the door. No doubt off to check the perimeter of the property.

She abandoned her task the moment she heard him reenter.

Peeking around the corner, she found him dressed in his everyday uniform of worn jeans and a dark T-shirt. He'd gone into the water wearing his brown shoes with the thick soles. Now he had on what she knew to be fairly pricey running shoes.

Was he a runner before his knee injury, or was he simply into having the best of everything, as Ty's son, Trey, had been? Ryan didn't strike her as the type of man to be overly concerned about impressing others, but who knew? People were hard to read sometimes.

Suddenly, she found herself intensely curious about him.

"Is everything okay?"

He nodded. "I contacted our host, and he informed me there's a gun club about a quarter mile down the road." Ryan tipped his head to the side, presumably indicating the direction of the property in question. "I checked the surrounding area. We're safe here."

"As safe as someone can be with live ammunition flying all over the place."

"I could find another place for us to go," he offered.

"No." The answer popped out of Kayla's mouth before her brain caught up.

This time at the lake, any lake, was what her heart

and soul needed. A refuge away from the heartbreak mixed in with the shambles of her life in Bentonville. "No," she said, gentling her tone. "I want to stay here." She gave him a tremulous smile. "Please don't stuff me in some soulless subdivision in Springdale. At least not for a couple days," she added with a wry smile.

Ryan gave a slow nod. "O-o-okay," he said, drawing the word out. "I may need to rethink our next location."

Kayla laughed then shook her head. She didn't want to cause this man any more work than she absolutely had to. "I was kidding. I can deal with subdivisions," she assured him.

"Good to know," he exhaled. "But for future reference, I'll do my best to keep us away from town, if you prefer. When we first spoke, you wanted to be close to the office, remember?"

She nodded. "I remember," she said definitively. "At the time I thought I'd be going into the office and making some sort of difference there. It's clear Michelle has everything under control, and given the fact Bill reached out to me after we made our appearance there, I suspect his informants were on the ball."

"Can you think of anyone other than the two you mentioned who may be close to Del?"

Kayla shook her head. "I've been racking my brain, but I wasn't there much over the past few years. My relationship with Del was friendly and cordial, but we didn't interact often until I married Ty."

"Understood."

Needing something to do, she gestured to the kitchen. "I'm hungry. How about you?"

He nodded slowly. "I could eat."

She opened the fridge and began to pull packages of sandwich fixings from it. "Let's talk about something else for a while," she suggested.

Ryan joined her in the small kitchen area. As he reached into a cabinet to pull down plates, he gave an agreeable nod. "Lady's choice."

"You grew up in Little Rock?"

"Didn't we cover this?" he asked, shooting her a sidelong glance.

"I'm rusty at making conversation that doesn't revolve around the Powers family," she replied stiffly. She could feel him watching her, but she kept her focus on arranging slices of bread on the plates. A long beat of silence passed, and for a moment, Kayla thought he was going to leave her dangling.

To her relief, he picked up the jar of mayonnaise and uncapped it as he spoke. "Did I tell you how I got into protective detail?"

"No." Cocking her head to the side, she eyed him curiously. "Is there a story?"

Ryan nodded. "I had a stepsister," he said gruffly.

His use of the past tense did not escape her notice. Kayla's shoulders tensed, but she forced herself to continue spreading thin layers of mayonnaise over each slice of bread. "A stepsister?" she asked, keeping her tone carefully neutral.

"Yes."

He reached for the package of ham and pulled it closer to him, then handed the sliced turkey to her. It didn't escape Kayla's notice that in a matter of days they'd already learned each other's preferences and habits.

"Talia," he said quietly. "Her name was Talia, but she went by Lia."

Kayla fought to keep her hands steady as she peeled off the thin slices of turkey breast and layered them onto the bread. "Pretty name."

"Yes. She was pretty, too."

She watched as he slapped half of the package of ham onto his own bread in a giant slab. She reached for the Swiss cheese and took out a thin slice, then handed it to him. "She must have been quite a bit younger than you," she observed. "Didn't you say you were in high school when your mother remarried?"

"Good memory," he said gruffly, accepting the package from her.

Tiring of the game of cat and mouse, Kayla turned to face him. "What happened to her?"

He placed two slices of cheese atop the pile of ham, then carefully zipped the package closed before tossing it aside. Instinctively, Kayla gripped the edge of the counter, bracing herself for whatever would come next in what she knew in her gut was the sad story. "What couldn't you protect her from?"

He didn't try to evade her amateur psychoanalysis, but he did not meet her gaze as he answered, "Herself."

"Oh, no." Her words came out in a hushed rush. "Did she hurt herself?"

She could tell by the way he held himself still that her deductions were close, if not precisely on the money. He shook his head. "Not exactly."

They stood frozen in place. The silence stretched so long Kayla wondered if she was going to have to cross-examine him to get the full story.

Beside her, Ryan heaved a full-body sigh then flipped the top piece of bread onto his sandwich, pressing down to meld his creation together. "She met some guy online," he said, picking up the plate and moving to one of the seats at the breakfast bar. "When my mother and her husband found out she was talking to the stranger on social media, they completely lost it. They tried to shut down all of her accounts, take away her phone, restrict about everything you could restrict in a fourteen-year-old's life."

"Fourteen," Kayla exhaled.

"Yeah." He cleared his throat then lifted one shoulder in a helpless shrug. "She lived with her dad most of the time, and she was pretty spoiled. Her mom wasn't particularly interested in being a full-time mother, and my mom…she was good at the mom thing."

"You seem to have turned out okay," Kayla teased with a small smile.

His lips quirked in response. "Lia didn't make it easy on her. When they did something she didn't like, she'd call me from the house phone and tattle on them." His gaze fixed on the lake beyond the windows. "I guess I was supposed to be her ally. Supposed to agree with her side of things. When they cut off her contact with the guy, she called them everything from monsters to fascists. I don't think she even knew what a fascist was other than it was something you weren't supposed to call somebody," he said wryly.

Needing to cut to the chase, she asked the direct question. "What happened to her?"

He kept his gaze fixed on the glistening lake. "She took off to meet him, of course."

From the deep timbre of his voice, she knew Lia's disappearance wasn't the end of the story. "He hurt her?"

Ryan nodded, his Adam's apple bobbing. "They found her body in the woods behind a rest stop on the interstate."

Kayla didn't ask for details about what had happened to her. She didn't need them. A young girl had been used and discarded. She reached over and gave his forearm a squeeze. "I am sorry," she said quietly.

He nodded in acknowledgment of her sympathy, then tore his gaze from the water. "I tried to work in cybercrimes for a while, but it hit too close to home. I couldn't be objective."

"You chose to protect people in other ways."

She moved to take the seat beside him, embarrassingly relieved to not have to look him in the eye.

"Yes." He was quiet for a moment, then picked up his sandwich but put it right back on the plate. "He'll have to go through me to get to you, Kayla."

"Thank you, but I don't want anyone to get to anybody," she countered.

"One way or another, this will come to a head," he warned her.

"Yes, it will."

He turned and eyed her warily. "You sound as if you're hoping it does."

"I am," she answered honestly. "I want Del caught

and questioned. I want to know why he shot me. I need to know if he had anything to do with Ty and Trey's deaths." She held his stormy gray gaze. "I hope to one day get back to living my life, whatever that means."

"I know you want answers—"

"No, I'll have answers," she interrupted. "I told you before and I'll tell you again, I won't hide forever. You and Ethan need to come up with a plan to flush Del out of the underbrush, or I will."

"Sounds like a threat," he growled.

"Not a threat," she said without the slightest hint of rancor. "A promise."

Chapter Eight

Ryan met with Ethan Scott a few hours after they moved into a town house in nearby Springdale. Kayla had mocked him mercilessly for the selection of the nondescript subdivision, but when he pointed out the relative anonymity provided by the identical units, she grudgingly admitted his plan was good. No one would look for her there.

The dairy bar not far from the Benton County Sheriff's Department was bustling. The roots of a scraggly tree had turned the asphalt driveway into chunks, but it provided a modicum of shade for customers waiting on their orders. He found Ethan leaning up against the side of his state-issued vehicle drawing deeply on a straw protruding from a foam cup.

"Hey," he said as he approached.

Ethan stopped sucking on his drink long enough to return the greeting and a jerk of his head. "Hey."

"How are things?" Ryan asked, falling in beside the other man.

Ethan shot him a look from under lowered eyebrows, took another pull on his straw, then muttered, "Quiet. Things are quiet."

Ryan nodded his understanding.

For most people quiet was good. Quiet was peaceful. Quiet meant all was well.

For a cop working an investigation where the brass continued to breathe fire, but the trail had gone cold, it was misery.

"I take it nothing came of Senator Powers's attempt to contact Mrs. Powers?" Ryan asked.

This time, Ethan didn't even remove the straw from his mouth when he shook his head.

"Man, you're gulping that thing down like it has all the answers," Ryan commented, amused by the other man's single-minded determination to drain whatever was in the cup.

"Pineapple milkshake," Ethan said from around the straw. He took another draw, then let it go with a sigh. "I thought it sounded gross at first, but Michelle's got me hooked on the darn things."

Ryan smirked. "Personally, I like the banana-cream ones."

Ethan nodded. "A respectable choice."

"No sightings of Del, I assume?" Ryan stated flatly.

Ethan returned to his milkshake lifeline. "You assume correctly."

"Does Michelle believe he's in contact with somebody at the firm?"

"Yes."

"Any suspects other than the two she named the day we went in there?"

Ethan shrugged. "No. I had a little informal chat with the two of them, but they're not giving anything up." He sighed and lowered the cup to his side. "I'm hanging on to the knowledge that I've never known a person to go underground and stay underground successfully. Certainly not one of these office types. You always have the paranoid paramilitary types who know how to go off the grid and live off in a lean-to in the woods, but they can never resist showing themselves eventually." He shrugged. "For all I know, Del Powers was one of those all along. Maybe he couched his survivalist tendencies in the safe I-like-to-fish-but-I'm-not-much-of-a-hunter kind of camouflage."

"We're pretty sure he is hunting Kayla, though," Ryan said grimly.

"My instincts tell me he hasn't gone away." Ethan turned and scanned the area beyond the razor wire fence that encircled the detention center attached to the sheriff's office. "Problem is there's too many places to hide in the hills."

"From what Kayla tells me, he's the patient sort. Who knows how long he'll wait?" Ryan mused grimly. He crossed his arms over his chest and joined Ethan in his perusal of the horizon beyond the secured facility. "Thoughts on using his father to flush him out?"

Ethan shot him a sidelong glance. "You want to be the one to suggest using a senator for bait?"

Ryan chuckled and shook his head. "No, sir."

"He's the one who's keeping the heat on the higher-ups. When I spoke to him about Kayla's impressions of the shooter, he dismissed the notion of it as ridiculous. Claims he's been in contact with Del, who has simply gone off on what the senator called 'one of his rambles' to get away from the discord over Tyrone Powers's will."

"If they've been in contact, then surely he has no opposition to telling Del we want to talk to him," Ryan countered.

"Senator Powers claims he's already informed Del of our interest in a conversation, and his son has assured him he will be in touch with us as soon as he returns from his trip." Ethan shot him a pointed glance. "Of course, neither of them could say when exactly that would be."

"And, in the meantime, the senator and his family have decamped to DC," Ryan said dryly.

Ethan heaved a sigh, then raised the cup to his mouth again. "Well, the man does have a job there, doesn't he?"

"That he does." Ryan ran a frustrated hand through his hair. "We moved again."

Ethan looked at him with interest. "Oh, yeah? How's it going?"

Ryan tipped his head to the side as if weighing his answer, but in the end, decided to admit he needed help. "She's restless. Anxious to get this resolved. Not only Del, but also the murders of her husband and stepson."

"I don't doubt it."

"I was wondering if maybe you and Michelle wanted to come to the place we're staying tonight. We could order in some food or I could cook. I think she's getting antsy."

"Tired of your company?" Ethan asked with a smirk.

"My company is scintillating," Ryan replied, deadpan. "But she's restless, and maybe between the four of us we can come up with some thoughts on how to draw Del out of the woods."

Ethan took a long pull on the straw that ended in a gurgle and a slurp. Heaving a disappointed sigh, he gave the now-empty cup a look as if it had betrayed him by not being bottomless. He then pushed away from the car. "Sounds good to me. Send me the details and let me know when you want us."

"Oh, and Kayla wanted me to ask about Harold Dennis," Ryan said before Ethan could get away.

Ethan let his head fall back and scrubbed a hand over his face. "Ah, Dennis," he sighed. "As somebody who was a lawyer, I can tell you there's nothing more miserable than having a lawyer in custody. Not only do they have a phalanx of other lawyers surrounding them at all times, but also it's hard to know exactly what to charge him with from one moment to the next. It's a veritable smorgasbord of choices."

"Isn't he the FBI's problem?" Ryan asked, straightening away from the vehicle and shoving his hands into the pockets of his jeans.

"Yes, which is why Michelle can probably give you better intel on him than me. He was her collar."

Ryan inclined his head in acknowledgment. "I forget she's a Fed." He shook his head. "What a mixed-up little world we have going on up here."

Ethan slapped him on the shoulder with a laugh. "Welcome to life in the Ozarks," he said sarcastically. "You thought Little Rock was a small town. Everybody is intertwined up here in one way or another, whether they're native or not." Ethan smirked and let his hand fall away as he started toward the door of the sheriff's department. He raised the hand in farewell.

Ryan stood watching as the other man trudged back into the building. It was clear the weight of the unsolved homicides weighed heavily on Ethan. The combination of pressure from within the ranks of the state police, the expectations of the public at large and the fact he was involved on a personal level had to make it all much more difficult.

Heading back to his car, Ryan thought that he would make every attempt to steal himself against the pull of Kayla Powers. The last thing he needed was to get any more enmeshed with these people than he already was. He had no intention of doing anything but finishing up his detail, and proving he was ready to come off desk duty back in Little Rock.

The town house they were staying in all week actually had more square footage than the cabin, but its vertical layout meant the space was narrow and deep rather than sprawling and spacious. The only way to avoid living on top of one another was to literally go upstairs to one of the bedrooms and spend their free hours cooped up there. Their companionable stay in the cabin had brought them together enough that it seemed churlish to take refuge on the second floor of the house.

Kayla had obviously decided she no longer felt the need to claim her own separate space. When he arrived back at the town house, he found her lounging on the living-room sofa flipping through options on the television. The temptation to join her was strong enough to force him to claim work responsibilities and head up to his room. After speaking with his superior and updating his assignment notes, he now had no choice but to shower, change for dinner and come downstairs to join her.

When he returned, he saw she'd changed into jeans and a pretty top with silver-gold thread running through the fabric. He assumed the change in wardrobe was for the sake of their company, not him, but he could appreciate it, nonetheless.

She sat perched on one of the stools at the kitchen island, a laptop open in front of her. She gave him a distracted hello as he came down the stairs. His brow furrowed as he approached the kitchen. "Hey," he returned. "Michelle and Ethan should be here soon."

She frowned at the screen. "I think Harold Dennis knows Del is somehow involved in Ty and Trey's deaths." She tapped the end of the stylus she was holding against her lips. A pucker formed between her eyebrows as she read whatever was on the screen.

"What makes you think he is?"

"Huh?" Then, as if realizing she'd actually spoken out loud to another human being, she jolted and slammed the lid of the laptop shut. "Oh. No reason... A gut feeling."

Ryan laughed and then circled the island to face her. "You're a terrible liar for a lawyer," he commented mildly.

She opened her mouth to protest, then snapped it shut. Pink spots appeared on her cheeks and she lowered her gaze for a moment, but then a bashful smile stretched her mouth. "I'm out of practice."

"What makes you say Harold Dennis suspected Del had something to do with your husband's death?"

"I'm not sure," she confessed.

He nodded. As a cop, he never discounted intuition. "Do you know what's giving you this feeling?" he persisted.

"No, it's—" She heaved a sigh then pried open the lid of the laptop again. When she turned it to face him, he could see she'd been marking up a document that looked like a transcript.

"What are you reading?"

The color on her cheeks deepened another shade. "Something I'm not supposed to."

He stared at her for a moment, weighing how he was supposed to respond to such a confession. "Do I want to know about it?" he asked cautiously, averting his gaze to the floor before he could register any of the verbiage on the screen.

"Maybe not at this point," she said quietly. "If I come across something concrete, I'll pass it along to Ethan and Michelle, but for your purposes, it's not need-to-know. I don't want to risk you crossing any ethical lines."

Ryan nodded then turned his gaze to the sliding door that led to the town house's minuscule patio, acting like he wasn't tempted to stare too hard at her or her ill-gotten documentation. "Thank you, I guess?"

Kayla chuckled. He heard the click of the laptop closing but didn't turn back until she rose from the stool. She placed the computer on the corner of the counter and walked toward the fridge. But he couldn't help eying the laptop like it was a snake about to strike. Something about the notion of her withholding information from him rankled, though he understood the reasoning behind it.

"Who's protecting who here?" he asked gruffly.

She pulled two bottles of water from the fridge, and handed one to him without asking. "You're willing to put yourself on the line to protect me physically. Why shouldn't I do what I need to do to protect your career and therefore your ability to continue protecting me?"

He uncapped the bottle as a burst of harsh laughter erupted from him. "Wow. You are a lawyer. I think your reasoning is somewhat convoluted."

Kayla smiled at him. "Not at all. Everyone has decided I need you to guard me from big, bad Del. You can't protect me if I put your job in jeopardy."

"Withholding information can be dangerous," he insisted.

"Withholding unsubstantiated suppositions helps us refrain from muddying the waters," she countered. "For the record, I ordered enough food to keep us full for the next week if Ethan and Michelle don't do their part to put it away."

He shook his head, unwilling to step into the web of her circular reasoning, but also frustrated by her ability to deflect. "Good. They should be here soon. I was half-afraid they'd want to get carryout from the dairy bar."

"I love the Daisy Dairy Bar," Kayla retorted, clearly affronted.

"Hey, I like a burger and rings as much as the next guy, but I have to admit I'm developing a general wariness for pineapple milkshakes. Apparently, they are addictive."

"That's the word on the street, though I have to say I'm partial to—"

A fist banging on the front door drew them both up short. Kayla slid off the stool, her eyes wide with surprise. Ryan felt a flash of annoyance. He might never get to hear exactly what Kayla Powers was partial to, and damn it, he wanted to know. But the shouts coming from the front of the town house quickly squashed his irritation.

Ethan and Michelle had arrived, but rather than the warm greetings of friends coming to share an evening in, they were both shouting about for them to unlock the door before they broke it down.

Both he and Kayla started for the front of the town house, but he quickly inserted himself in front of her. "Stay in the living room," he ordered. "Let me see what's going on."

He didn't wait to see if she wanted to argue with him. There didn't seem to be time. Two armed agents were standing on the doorstep threatening to bust into the place, and he had to find out why.

"Sergeant Ryan Hastings, Arkansas State Police," he shouted back. "Identify yourselves."

The pounding ceased as abruptly as it started and there was a beat of silence before Michelle answered him. "Special Agent Michelle Fraser, FBI, and Lieutenant Ethan Scott, ASP-CID."

"Why are you pounding on the door?" Ryan demanded as he approached it, leaning down to touch the sidearm he had strapped to his ankle beneath his jeans.

"Are you both okay?" Ethan countered.

Ryan straightened halfway, gun in hand, but a quick

glance through the peephole confirmed the only people standing on the threshold were indeed Ethan and Michelle. In one fluid movement, he returned his firearm to its holster and disengaged the locks as he rose again. He yanked open the door and ushered them in. The second they crossed into the foyer, he slammed the door shut and locked it. "What's going on?"

Michelle held an enormous brown paper bag with handles. It was emblazoned with the logo of a local food-delivery service and appeared to be loaded to the top with carryout containers.

"Where have you been? Did he ring the doorbell?" Ethan demanded, brandishing a piece of lined paper torn from a spiral-bound notebook. A scrap of silver duct tape with frayed edges was stuck to the top of the page.

"We've been here waiting for you," Ryan said impatiently. "And no. No one rang the bell. Why?"

"This was taped to the bag and sitting on the welcome mat," Ethan replied, waving the note in the general direction of their dinner delivery.

"Wha—"

Neatly drawn black marker letters glared back at him.

YOU TRADED LAKEFRONT PROPERTY FOR THIS?

"Holy—" Ryan blew a soft swear out on a gust of air. "Someone knows you're here," Ethan concluded.

Ryan shot him a glare he hoped conveyed how little

he appreciated statements of the obvious. "Excellent deduction, Holmes."

Michelle raised both eyebrows and stepped between the two men as if she and a bag full of fragrant food could shield Ethan from sarcasm. "Let's all take a breath," she said in a measured, but firm tone. "Someone knows where this order was being delivered. They don't necessarily know who is here."

"If it was the food-delivery driver, I want my tip back," Kayla said, stepping into the foyer.

"Did you order the food?" Ethan asked without preamble.

"What? Yeah. Why?" she asked, eyes narrowing.

Ryan swiveled to face her. "Did you use your own name or credit card?"

She shook her head as if to clear it. "No, I used the account you had me set up," she replied, her tone shaky. "The one in Frank Farmer's name."

"Frank Farmer?" Michelle repeated, her brow crinkling. "Why does that name sound familiar?"

"Kevin Costner's character in *The Bodyguard*. It was a joke," Kayla said briskly. "What's happening?"

Ryan felt the intensity of her stare down to his bones. She addressed the question to him, rather than to Ethan, who still held the note. "We don't know it was him." He met his friend's gaze and knew he was grasping at straws.

"What was who?" Kayla demanded.

Ryan snatched the note from Ethan before Kayla spotted it and could do the same. How had Powers figured it out? The only people who were fully clued in were the four of them, a couple of local deputies who had helped with checking locations and Ryan's superior.

The *how* didn't matter now. Once Kayla saw this note, she would know his brilliant master plan for keeping her safe by keeping her moving had failed. He had failed.

"There was a note attached to the food delivery," Michelle reported. She pulled the long strip of receipt stapled to the bag closer to her face to inspect it. "The restaurant receipt shows the name as Frank Farmer."

"But somehow he knows who Frank Farmer is, and where Frank Farmer has been staying," Ethan said grimly.

"He?" Kayla interjected. "He, as in Del?" she asked, turning to Ryan for confirmation. "How?"

Ryan's jaw tensed, but there was no point in trying to put her off. "I don't know how, but yes. Someone knows we've been moving from property to property, and we have to assume that person is Del Powers."

Michelle lowered the sack of food to the floor by its handles. "Before we get too far afield with this, I suggest we call for backup and another dinner."

"Another dinner?" Kayla asked, her tone bewildered.

"It's probably some fairly advanced paranoia on my part," Michelle admitted with a grimace of a smile, "but I don't think I want to eat this. If neither of you heard the delivery, or anyone else outside before we arrived, we have no way of knowing if he tampered with it."

"He must have intercepted the driver," Kayla whispered, her gaze falling to the bag.

Ethan pulled his cell from his pocket and speed-dialed

a contact. "Hey, it's Scott here. I need a patrol car parked outside the address I'm sending to you. Someone has the drop on where Mrs. Powers is staying."

Ryan's gut churned as he turned over every move they'd made in his mind. Where had they slipped up? Was he the weak link? Had someone followed him back to the town house after he met with Ethan?

Ethan ended the call with a sigh. Nudging the enormous bag of food that would go uneaten. "I asked Sheriff Stenton to have the deputy he's sending over pick up pizza for himself and for us."

"Are we staying here tonight?" Kayla asked.

Again, she turned to him for confirmation and Ryan wanted to personally hunt down Del Powers and make him pay for the frightened look in her eyes.

"No sense in going anywhere else," he answered gruffly. "We'll have a deterrent outside—"

"And three armed agents inside," Michelle interjected.

"Armed?" Kayla turned to look at her friend quizzically. "You brought your gun to dinner?"

"Kayla, sweets, we're cops," Michelle said in a cajoling tone. "We don't go anywhere unprepared." She wrapped an arm around Kayla's waist and turned her back toward the kitchen.

Ryan met Ethan's gaze and gave a defiant lift of his chin even as he fought back his body's natural inclination to blush.

"We need to come up with another plan," Ethan said quietly.

As if Ryan needed to have it explained to him. He couldn't resist lashing out. "No kidding."

"I'm not criticizing," Ethan said, raising his hands in surrender. "I was trying to remind you there are four of us here, and among us we have plenty of brainpower to figure out where this went sideways."

"I've already narrowed it down," Ryan said grimly.

Ethan gave him a wan smile. "Me, too."

Somehow, his superior had to have given up enough information for Powers to track them down. How and why, Ryan didn't know. He'd have time to figure it out later. For now, he had to keep his focus on his primary.

Kayla was going to be even more resistant than she'd been at the start. He'd been able to use the scare of the shots fired at the lake to his advantage for a couple of days, but this turn of events would turn the tide against ducking and hiding. He'd learned enough about her over the course of the past week and a half to know the clock had already been ticking.

Kayla Powers was not the type to stand down for long.

Chapter Nine

Kayla allowed the conversation to swirl around her. In the hour since Michelle and Ethan's arrival, she'd found it difficult to do more than ask the most rudimentary questions.

Everyone had an opinion. They needed to move tonight. No, morning would be soon enough. Perhaps someplace out of state? Could Michelle's contacts at the FBI help find a place outside of Del Powers's comfort zone? Surely there was a safe house they could use.

Each of them had questions, but no one asked her opinion.

Where should she go? What were the odds the note had been left by someone other than Del? Was Senator Powers involved? Was all of this tied to Harold Dennis's money-laundering schemes? Was Harold behind Del's attack on Kayla? Had Harold, Del and the senator concocted an elaborate scheme to take control of the Powers fortune? Were they cold-blooded enough to kill their own family to secure their futures?

They talked over each other, voices rising with each objection and growing more strident as their speculation dove deeper. Kayla sat quietly at the town house's small dining table, while all around her the people she'd grown closest to talked about her like she was some kind of rare porcelain doll they needed to store in an airtight, unbreakable box until they deemed the world safe enough for her to emerge.

Inside she seethed.

At her friends. At Ryan. She saved a good bit of her inner vitriol for Del, of course. And in fairness, she added in Harold Dennis, Bill Powers and the world in general. Afraid to open her mouth for fear of unleashing her rage, she sat quietly and stared at a spot beyond her untouched slice of pizza.

It was impossible to eat when she was biting her tongue.

But no one seemed to notice her reticence. Or maybe they were too keyed up to tune in to her feelings. It was just as well. If she let them run their course, eventually, they would run out of steam and look to her for some sort of validation.

Then she'd tell them what she would do.

"What if we look for someplace in a more metropolitan area?" Michelle suggested. "Dallas? Tulsa? Kansas City? Someplace where it's easier to get lost in a crowd. Someplace not located directly in the Powers family's backyard."

"Someplace out of their sphere of influence," Ethan chimed in, pointing a half-eaten pizza crust at Michelle as if it helped hammer home the point.

"Cities present a whole other set of variables. If you're going to stay regional, I'd almost rather we head for Little Rock. At least I know the lay of the land there and would have plenty of backup."

"Good point," Ethan conceded, slumping back in his seat and dropping the uneaten crust onto his plate. He glanced over at Michelle. "What do you think of Little Rock?"

"Personally, or for Kayla?" she asked. But it was clear from her tone the question was rhetorical.

They fell silent for a moment. Ryan reached into the pizza box for another slice. He was about to lower the lid when he caught sight of her plate and frowned. "You're not eating."

A sneer twisted the corners of her lips, and a rush of indignation heated her blood. "I was sitting here waiting for one of y'all to tell me how to do it," she replied in a tone as cool as her blood was hot.

All conversation stopped. Michelle and Ethan turned to look at her, then down at her untouched plate. Michelle met her gaze again, her expression troubled. Kayla could almost see the other woman weighing whether she needed to be in friend mode or put on her lawyer hat.

"No one is telling you what to do," Ryan replied in what she assumed was his best hostage-negotiations tone.

"For the past thirty minutes the three of you have discussed how best to 'handle' me right in front of me," she snapped, raising her arms to be certain everyone appreciated her use of air quotes.

"We were talking about security," Ryan countered.

"My security," she replied. "The guarding of my body.

Free Books Claim Card
Say "Yes" to More Books!

HARLEQUIN Reader Service —**Here's how it works:**

Accepting your 2 free books and free gift (gift valued at approximately $10.00 retail) places you under no obligation to buy anything. You may keep the books and gift and return the shipping statement marked "cancel." If you do not cancel, approximately one month later we'll send you more books from the series you have chosen, and bill you at our low, subscribers-only discount price. Harlequin® Romantic Suspense books consist of 4 books each month and cost just $5.49 each in the U.S. or $6.24 each in Canada, a savings of at least 12% off the cover price. Harlequin Intrigue® Larger-Print books consist of 6 books each month and cost just $6.49 each in the U.S. or $6.99 each in Canada, a savings of at least 13% off the cover price. It's quite a bargain! Shipping and handling is just 50¢ per book in the U.S. and $1.25 per book in Canada*. You may return any shipment at our expense and cancel at any time by contacting customer service — or you may continue to receive monthly shipments at our low, subscribers-only discount price plus shipping and handling.

▲ If offer card is missing write to: Harlequin Reader Service, P.O. Box 1341, Buffalo, NY 14240-8531 or visit www.ReaderService.com ▲

BUSINESS REPLY MAIL
FIRST-CLASS MAIL   PERMIT NO. 717   BUFFALO, NY

POSTAGE WILL BE PAID BY ADDRESSEE

HARLEQUIN READER SERVICE
PO BOX 1341
BUFFALO NY 14240-8571

NO POSTAGE
NECESSARY
IF MAILED
IN THE
UNITED STATES

My person. As if it didn't come with a functioning brain included in the package."

"Now, Kay—" Michelle began.

"No." Kayla turned her glare on her friend. "You were doing it, too. Talking about me like I'm some kind of valuable painting, or delicate statue you have to tuck away in a vault somewhere."

"We know you aren't those things," Michelle said, her manner forthright, "but the issue at hand is protecting you. Your person, as you said. Including your brain," she added with a lift of one perfectly groomed eyebrow. "No one is excluding you from the discussion."

"No one has asked for my input," Kayla pointed out.

Ethan had the good grace to look down at his own empty plate before busying himself with liberating another slice of pizza from the box.

"I believe we all assumed we were brainstorming," Ryan said gruffly.

"I'll refrain from repeating the old bit about assumptions and move on to telling you what happens next," she said, her voice taut.

There was a moment. A split second where the other three seated at the table froze for a heartbeat. The conversation resumed when Michelle cocked her head to the side and asked, "Yes? We're listening."

"I'm moving back to the house on Table Rock," she announced.

The words came out of her mouth before she'd even given the decision much thought, but she wasn't admitting as much to this crew. Not when they were stumbling over one another to voice their objections. She let them go for a minute, sitting still, but feeling surprisingly serene about her decision.

And while she was grateful for all the time and effort Ryan had put into his plan to keep them moving, it obviously wasn't the right answer. Unless she was willing to leave the area, possibly even the state, someone would likely have eyes on her. And she couldn't walk away now. Not with Ty's murder unsolved and his child growing in her belly.

No. Her heart had spoken. Or maybe it was her gut. Either way, she knew in her bones she needed to be on her own turf to see this through.

When their objections spluttered to a stop, she sat up straighter and folded her hands on the edge of the table, pushing the plate away a few centimeters. Ryan's gaze dropped to the uneaten pizza as if she'd issued an ultimatum. And maybe, in a way, she was. After all, they couldn't force her to accept their help.

"Listen, I appreciate all of…this," she said, gesturing to the town house, then catching Ryan's eye. "But it's not working. Someone is watching us. Whether it's Del or not, I can't say, but it's safe to assume he has eyes on us one way or another."

He lifted his chin, the muscle in a corner of his jaw working as he formulated his response.

"Ryan, it's not working," she repeated, gentling her tone. "They know where we are and they know where we've been."

He broke eye contact, tucking his chin to his chest as he nudged the plate toward her again. "Doesn't mean we should make you a sitting duck," he grumbled.

"I'm willing to do whatever we need to do to make you feel better about me being there," she said, keeping her tone even, but firm. "We can upgrade the security system."

"A new system would be the bare minimum you'd have to do," he countered.

"We can make it top-of-the-line," she assured him. "You're welcome to come and stay there as well. The place is enormous."

His head jerked up. "Not a plus in this situation," he informed her. "We need less space. There's too much out there. It's uncontained."

"Exactly my point. I am also uncontainable," she declared. "I'm a human being trying to live my life. If you want to keep me under wraps, you're going to have to arrest me first."

Ryan and Ethan exchanged a glance. Both Kayla and Michelle leaned in, on high alert.

"What?" Michelle demanded.

"Nothing," Ethan replied. He took an enormous bite of his slice, no doubt to avoid having to answer their interrogation.

"It wasn't nothing," Kayla growled. "Tell me, or I'll refuse protection entirely."

"You shouldn't use your life as a bargaining chip," Ryan retorted.

"The point being, it's my life. If anyone gets to use it as a bargaining chip, it's me. What have you two been discussing? Behind my back?"

"There's been no discussion," Ethan said through stuffed cheeks.

"There was something there," Michelle insisted. "I thought we were all supposed to be on the same team here. Team Kayla alive." She sent a pointed look at Kayla herself. "Part of being a team means no pronouncements from on high. No backroom double-dealing," she said turning her gaze to the two men. "If we're going to figure this out as a team, we need to discuss options, not argue."

"Hard not to argue when three out of four of the people sitting at this table are lawyers," Ryan grumbled.

Kayla had to smile at his assessment. Turning back to Michelle, she said, "I wasn't making a pronouncement from on high," she said. "I was simply saying I wanted to go back to my own house. I don't think it's an unreasonable request given the fact we know trying to evade detection has not worked."

"Your house is too exposed," Ryan said gravely.

"Not to mention it's not actually technically your house. Senator Powers still holds interest in it, and that interest could mean Del has some rights to it, too," Ethan reminded her.

"I haven't forgotten," Kayla assured them. "I can assure you Bill Powers isn't going to risk his career by coming anywhere near me or northwest Arkansas until the stories about Tyrone's death and Harold Dennis's financial indiscretions have faded entirely," she insisted.

"I'm still wanting to know what the look meant," Michelle said, pinning Ethan with a penetrating stare. "Given the tenor of the conversation, I can't help wondering if you're playing with the notion of arresting my client."

"Arresting me?" Kayla said, snapping to attention.

"Not for real," Ethan said, holding up both hands placatingly. "But you have to admit, it wouldn't be a bad idea to let people think you've been taken into custody."

"Wouldn't be a bad idea?" Michelle growled.

"Are you kidding me with this?" Kayla demanded.

"Were you going to say anything to me about this, or were you planning on popping in and cuffing her without a shred of hard evidence?" Michelle said, glaring at Ethan.

"Is this some sort of asinine keep-her-under-wraps-at-all-costs sort of ploy?" Kayla asked Ryan as she rose from her seat.

Both men raised their hands in a gesture commonly used when a guy was about to deploy the old calm-down tactic, but neither was reckless or brave enough to actually utter those two fatal words.

"It was only an idea we tossed around," Ethan said, digging his hole a little deeper.

"Not a serious one," Ryan added quickly, shooting daggers at his friend and colleague. He almost saved himself with a single glare, but then he opened his mouth again. "But you have to admit, it would be a pretty good way of keeping you safe. Let the Powerses think we've caught the culprit…"

"They'd come crawling out of the woodwork the minute word leaked you were in custody," Ethan added.

"Then we set something up to get Del to implicate himself," Ryan said, nodding.

Ethan grimaced even as he nodded in agreement. "At least in the shooting at the lake house," he amended.

Kayla gaped at them, incredulous. "And exactly how long were you planning to keep me in custody?"

"As long as it takes," Ethan replied, his expression grim.

"Oh, you can't be serious," Michelle cried.

"I've heard some cock-a-doodle schemes, but how exactly do you think you're going to get someone to confess to a double homicide when you have a suspect in custody?" Kayla demanded. "Why wouldn't they want me to take the fall?" She threw her arms open wide. "Heck, they'd probably throw a parade for you."

"You'd be surprised how often guilty parties give themselves away once they think their getaway is assured," Ethan said soberly.

Beside her, Michelle stiffened in her seat. Kayla cocked her head, staring down at her friend and attorney in stunned disbelief. "You aren't about to buy in to this plan, are you?"

To her credit, Michelle shook her head with brain-sloshing ferocity. "No. But I do have to tell you, Ethan's right. Most people who think they've gotten away with a crime feel compelled to flaunt it in some way."

"It would be a way for you to ensure you are able to secure your late husband's legacy," Ryan said quietly.

Kayla gripped the back of her chair, shocked disbelief pulsing through her. Ignoring the thrum of her blood pounding in her ears, she stared down at the man she thought she'd come to know over the past week and a half. Her rage barely contained, she spoke through clenched teeth.

"If I'm no longer willing to move from one short-term rental to another, you can bet your badge I'm not about to give birth to Tyrone's baby in prison, Sergeant."

She bit off the last syllable and turned on her heel to stalk from the room. Unfortunately, the town house's open-concept floor plan didn't lend itself well to dramatic exits. She made it to the foot of the stairs before an explosion of voices tore through the aftermath of her pronouncement.

Ethan spoke first. "Nobody said anything about prison... Wait. She's pregnant?"

"Tyrone's baby?" Michelle asked, her tone dazed.

"What the— No way," Ethan said. "I can't even do the math."

Chairs scraped laminate flooring and Ryan let out a loud groan. "Oh, man. Kayla, wait," he called after her.

She reached the top of the stairs as Michelle barked a breathless but commanding "Hey!"

Closing her eyes, Kayla stilled, but did not turn back to face her friend.

"Are you really?" Michelle asked, her tone softening as she trotted up the steps.

Kayla could feel the other woman standing firm and unflinching at her back. "Yeah, I am."

"Are we happy about this?" Michelle whispered.

Kayla couldn't help but smile at the solidarity implied by the other woman's use of the plural pronoun. Glancing tentatively over her shoulder, she let the smile grow a fraction before she answered with an unwavering, "Yes."

Michelle gave a single decisive nod at the pronouncement. "Well, wow. Okay, then." She gave a huff of a laugh. "Okay. Well, come back downstairs. I promise not to let Ethan arrest you."

"Like you could stop me," Ethan mumbled, flashing Kayla a shamefaced smile as she reached the bottom of the staircase. "It was only a spitball."

"Yeah, well, it fell short," she retorted. Without bothering to look at Ryan, she asked, "What do we need to do to beef up security enough to make you feel comfortable with the move back to Table Rock Lake?"

"You know a good way to fence off waterfront?" he asked.

"You were okay with us being on Beaver Lake this past week," she reminded him.

Ryan quirked an eyebrow. "I was okay with it because I believed no one knew we were there. Now I know different."

"Proving that hiding from him isn't the answer," she countered.

"We've been through this," he growled.

She crossed her arms over her chest and lifted her chin. "Either you're coming with me or I'm going alone. It's up to you, Sergeant."

"You're not going alone," he barked.

"Then tell me what we need to have put in place. I'm booking rooms at a B and B I know in Eureka Springs for three nights, then I'm moving back home."

She felt a twinge at calling the lake house *home*. It wasn't the house she shared with Tyrone. The house and the parcels of land surrounding it weren't even hers to call her own. They belonged to the Powers family, and would in perpetuity, given the complex trusts put in place by Ty's father. But her child would be a Powers, and as Ty's only living offspring, they would inherit his share in the estate along with the personal wealth Ty had amassed on his own.

"I have ample resources, Ryan. Tell me what's needed, and we'll get people on it first thing in the morning."

"Unless you have enough cash to build a force field, it will be nothing more than a drop in the bucket," he countered.

Ethan and Michelle's heads swiveled like spectators at a tennis match, but they said nothing.

She pursed her lips. "Perhaps I should speak to someone at the state police about finding a more cooperative agent to work on my security detail?"

"Stop threatening me," he said, taking a step closer.

Kayla held his gaze, closing the distance between them until they stood toe-to-toe. "Stop trying to bully me."

A growl of frustration ripped from his throat, but he didn't back down. "I am not trying to bully you. I'm trying to make you face reality."

"Face reality," she repeated, blinking up at him in disbelief. "You seriously think you can give me a reality check?"

Her voice rose on the last bit. Michelle hastened to her side and exhaled, "Uh oh."

Ryan ran a hand through his thick, russet hair. "No, I didn't intend—"

But it was too late. "Face reality," she said with a sneer. "Well, maybe you're right, because it was pretty darn surreal to walk into my family room and find my husband and his son shot dead."

"Kayla—" Ryan began.

"And you know what's a real trip?" she interrupted. "Standing up against people who've intimidated me since the moment we met. But I did because my husband wanted me to be the custodian of his precious law firm."

"I know you have—" he said, but was cut off again.

"To weather the investigation, speculation and social ostracism in the days and weeks after. To have no one but Michelle by my side as I grieved as quietly and decorously as I could because heaven forbid I made a scene," she raged.

"And you did," he insisted.

"Suspicion clings like the stink on a skunk." In her agitation, the drawl she tried so hard to modulate came creeping in like kudzu. "I spent night after night alone in a hotel room drinking myself to sleep, wondering how I'd ever measure up. But you know what? It turns out I didn't have to," she said, lifting her chin in defiance. "Because there was nothing to measure up to," she continued, undeterred.

Ryan tried to interject in a soothing tone. "Kayla, we know—"

"It turns out the people I thought were so much better than me were nothing but common criminals. Harold Dennis with his stealing and double-dealing. Bill Powers, who only comes around when he wants to soak people for money. And Del…"

She let loose with a harsh, self-deprecating laugh.

"Quiet, good-natured Delray Powers, who takes

cheap shots at unarmed women, and possibly murdered his own uncle and cousin." She threw up her hands. "You're right, Ryan, this cannot be reality. Someone had to have made all this up because it's too bizarre to be real."

"But it is," Michelle interjected.

Kayla's head whipped around. She'd been so focused on confronting Ryan Hastings and his plans to bulldoze her, she'd forgotten they had an audience. She met her best friend's eyes, then blinked. As always, the worry and compassion she saw in Michelle's steadfast gaze grounded her.

"But it is," she agreed in a whisper.

"And you've made it through all of it, all on your own," her friend continued. "But you aren't alone, Kayla. We're here to help you. Let us help you."

Kayla swallowed the hot lump of emotion lodged in her throat. "All I want is to go home."

Michelle pursed her lips as if weighing the demand, then nodded. She turned to Ryan, her expression serious and her tone unyielding. "As my client said, she has money at her disposal, Sergeant Hastings. Let's spend some of it to make the Powers family estate on Table Rock Lake as secure as it can be."

Ryan nodded his assent and pulled out his phone. "Get out your credit card," he grumbled as he scrolled through his contacts. "If you're going to go bragging about your money, then I'm going to be crowing about how much of it I spent."

Chapter Ten

Ryan kicked a rock and sent it tumbling across the leaf-strewn ground. It came to rest at the base of a spindly pine tree, and so did he. Planting his hands on his hips, he turned to survey the property from ten feet beyond the invisible perimeter protected by the new security system installed at the Powers's lake house. Truthfully, he was happy to be out of the frilly B&B.

It was too close, as far as he was concerned, but there wasn't much he could do to secure the exterior.

The interior, on the other hand...

He smirked, recalling Kayla's furrowed brow as she tried to follow the directions for accessing the smart home features. She made the technician repeat the various voice prompts three times. On the last attempt, she made the man turn on the voice-recording feature and run through each option. Then, she cross-examined the poor guy on the capabilities of each and every application.

Ryan had tossed his duffel into one of the upstairs guest rooms. It was two doors down from the primary bedroom. Far enough to give her the privacy she craved, but close. Maybe not as close as he'd like, given the massive scale of the place. But close enough.

Cutting through the woods, he circled the house, heading for the lakefront. When he broke from the trees onto the neatly maintained stretch of lawn, he made a mental note to see if he could get hold of an aerial view of the estate. If he was going to try to keep her safe out there, he needed a feel for the entire property from every possible angle.

Things had been quiet since the night of their intercepted food delivery. Too quiet.

Ryan had the uneasy feeling their every move had been watched and noted, but for the life of him, he couldn't pick up any trace of Del Powers in the area. Huffing from frustration more than exertion, he crossed the sloping expanse of grass, half-wishing he had at least one more rock to kick. He'd stepped onto the native stone pavers leading down to the swimming dock and boat slips when his phone rang.

"Hastings," he said in a brusque, business-like bark, even though the name on the screen informed him the caller was Ethan.

The lieutenant must have been in a similar mood because he didn't bother with even the most cursory greeting. "What do you think about leaking the fact Senator Powers's son might be a person of interest in the deaths of his uncle and cousin?"

Ryan stopped in his tracks and let out a low whistle. "I think you're a braver man than I am. Why not try poking the hornet's nest before yanking it down and wearing it as a hat?"

"Can't be any worse than the heat I'm getting from the inside. I swear, the only person not calling to badger me about this case daily is Kayla."

Both men fell silent for a moment, unspoken questions and hypotheses as to why the victim's widow wasn't heading up the line of people pushing the lead investigator on the case swirling around them.

"I think she's still in shock," Ryan said at last, breaking the tension. "I know she speaks to Michelle every day. And her therapist from Briarwood. Maybe she's getting enough information about the investigation from Michelle to keep her satisfied? Besides, I think she trusts you," he added after a thoughtful pause.

Ethan was quiet on the other end of the call. "Yeah. No. You're right. I'm grasping at straws." At last, he sighed. "I'll call if I come up with a better approach."

Ryan ended the call and made his way down to the dock. He stood with his feet spread wide, listening to the soft slap of lake water against the hulls of the boats docked in the nearby slips. He glanced over. The passenger compartment of the slick ski boat he assumed belonged to Trey Powers was covered with a canvas cover.

He thought about the girl who'd either fallen or been knocked off the boat as he stared out at the lake. The water was a near-impossible blue in the bright sunlight. A steady breeze out of the northwest sent ripples skittering across the surface. The day was warm, but the sticky humidity of summer was fading. Months had passed since Mallory Murray had gone missing, but there'd never be any resolution to the case. Not unless one of the people who'd crowded onto the back of the boat changed their story, which wasn't likely to happen. Accident or not, no one had bothered to pull poor Mallory out of the lake.

And now, the murder of the man who'd left her for dead could possibly go unsolved. He totally understood Ethan's desperation. The higher-ups were not going to be satisfied until he brought in the killer—or, at least, the person who'd paid the killer—wrapped in a bow. But trying to bait the son of a sitting senator into showing himself was probably not the best path to justice a man with career ambitions could take.

"Hey."

Kayla's voice jolted him from his thoughts. He turned to find her standing on the edge of the terrace, hand on her hips and a curious tilt to her head.

"Hey," he replied, pivoting to face her. "You shouldn't be out here like this," he admonished. Hurrying up the stone path, he tried to figure out the best angle to place his body between her and whoever might be watching them from the edge of the waterfront.

She glanced down, then back up at him with a puzzled expression. "What do you mean? I'm wearing pants, aren't I?"

He quickened his pace, fully intending to hustle her back into the safety of the house. "You're standing up there exposed for everyone to see," he half-shouted, hooking a thumb over his shoulder.

By the time he reached her, both of Kayla's eyebrows were riding high. "I hate to break this to you, but we're the only people out here. Well, other than Deputy Warren, but I doubt he can see me parked at the gate."

He huffed, ignoring the twinge of pain in his knee as he climbed the last few feet. "You know what I mean," he grumbled, catching her by the elbow and not breaking stride.

"Okay, if you're going to pull the caveman moves, I'd appreciate it if you'd either toss me over your shoulder or drag me by the hair, because my arm is sore and—"

He released her as if she was radioactive. A chiding voice in the back of his head reminded him her arm had healed, but logic didn't play into it. He wasn't there to inflict harm, he was there to protect her from it. They stood staring at one another, as stubborn and entrenched as TV news anchors in a tug-of-war of wills.

"Your arm is fine," he accused, narrowing his eyes, challenging her to say otherwise.

Kayla's chin popped up, but her mouth curved into a smile. "It is. Thanks for asking."

"Kayla," he said in a low, warning tone.

"Ryan," she countered. He gave an involuntary grunt, and her smile grew exponentially. "Come inside. I have a surprise for you, and I want to ask a favor."

She didn't wait for his response. Kayla Powers was a woman who'd grown accustomed to getting her way. As he watched her walk toward the glass doors that opened onto the terraced patio, he felt a sharp stab of recognition.

Suddenly, he was nineteen again, standing bewildered in the upstairs hallways of his mother's massive home in Little Rock. He'd skipped an afternoon class to come home for the weekend, hoping to surprise his mom and spend some time hanging out with a couple friends from high school. But rather than the warm welcome he'd been anticipating, he'd found himself listening in shocked disbelief as the woman who'd raised him on the paltry salary of a chain-hotel, front-desk clerk fired her assistant for not hanging his stepfather's dry cleaning in his closet properly.

"Ryan?" Kayla called to him, jolting him from the memory.

He met her gaze. But unlike the cool disparagement he'd seen in his mother's eyes that day, he saw only concern, warmth and maybe a hint of mischief in Kayla's. "Oh. Yeah. Right," he murmured.

Ryan tried to maintain an air of indifference as he crossed the massive patio with its built-in firepit and brick pizza oven, but his knee was aching and his pride was wounded. This woman played him too easily. She got under his skin. He needed to be on his guard— not only for her, but also with her.

"What is it?" he asked, injecting a note of perturbed impatience into the question in hopes of putting her on her heels as well.

It worked. Kayla blinked in surprise, then her forehead creased with worry. "Is your knee hurting?"

Damn if the woman wasn't the most frustrating mass of contradictions. How could someone so oblivious to her own peril be so attuned to someone else's pain? He fell back on his standard response. "A twinge. I'm fine." He nodded for her to precede him into the house. "What did you want to ask me?"

She shook her head as she crossed the threshold. "Surprise first." Turning back to face him, she said loudly, "Play Ryan's song."

A disembodied voice replied from an invisible speaker. "Playing Ryan's song."

Before he could process what was happening, Whitney Houston's voice blared from the whole-home audio system, belting out the crescendo of the song she'd resurrected for the movie *The Bodyguard*.

He shook his head in mock dismay, doing his best not to crack a smile, but it was not an easy thing to do when bombarded by professions of unending love.

She reached for the high note at the climax, and their eyes met. Seeing the devilish delight lighting Kayla's face made it impossible for him to remain stoic. Grinning back at her, he shook his head, not even attempting to speak over the soaring declarations.

Then, as if she'd tuned in to the lyrics for the first time, Kayla's eyes widened, and her cheeks colored. Ryan didn't bother trying to stifle his laughter as he watched her succumb to the mortification of possible misinterpretation.

"Stop," she shouted over the music.

But the song continued to play.

"Stop the music," she ordered again.

But Whitney sang on.

"Mute," she shouted in frustration.

The command did the trick. Silence roared through the cavernous house, and for an uncomfortable moment, Ryan almost wished she'd let the song play to its conclusion. At least then, the echoes would be filled with wistful longing rather than gut-wrenching emotion. Hoping to ease the tension, he tore his gaze from her flushed cheeks and looked up at the ceiling as if searching out the concealed speakers.

"Wow, no one has made a joke about me being Kevin Costner in at least five minutes," he said in a bored drawl.

To his relief, Kayla laughed. "You have to admit it made for a good entrance."

"Now I'll expect nothing less each time I walk through a door," he answered, making a point of meeting her gaze again. "I take it the song was my surprise. What is the favor?"

With a huff, Kayla blew a lock of blond hair from her cheek. "I want you to walk down to the mailbox with me."

"The mailbox?" he repeated, puzzled. "Do you need to have something sent?"

She shook her head, but she couldn't quite meet his eyes. "No, I want to go check the mail."

"You expecting a big check or something?" he joked, then, with a frown added, "Do people even have checks anymore?"

"Yes, they do, and no, I am not expecting one." She gestured for him to follow, then took off in front of him again.

Ryan caught up to her in two strides, but this time he didn't make a grab for her arm. "I don't get it," he said as she made a beeline down the corridor leading to the front entrance. "What's in the mail?"

"Nothing's in the mail," she countered as they reached the heavy double doors.

He watched as she disarmed the alarm with a few taps of the keypad, then twisted the locks. She reached for the handle, and he stepped closer.

"Hey, you going to tell me what's going on here?"

Kayla pressed her lips together, and for a moment he thought she might bolt without explanation. He caught the edge of the heavy door as it started to swing into the foyer, his forearm effectively blocking her way until he was given a more satisfactory answer.

"Kayla?"

"I was checking the mailbox the day he shot me," she answered, her gazed fixed on the middle distance beyond the door.

"The day Del shot you?"

She nodded.

"What were you looking for in the mail?" he asked, hoping for some more clarity.

"Nothing," she answered with a huff of impatience. "Would you stop fixating on the mail?"

"I will if you explain to me why we need to go check the mailbox," he retorted, pushing the door closed and leaning into it, his palm flat on the polished wood, his fingers splayed wide.

Kayla tucked her chin to her chest, and for the briefest moment, he thought she might concede the fight. Then, she jerked her head up and glared at him.

"It's a thing, okay? Once I checked out of Briarwood, I started doing it daily. The walk down the drive and back was my exercise."

He tactfully refrained from mentioning the state-of-the-art home gym he'd spotted on the lower level of the house.

She exhaled dramatically and her shoulders drooped as if he was wringing the information out of her. "It was nice. It was a nice walk down to the road. I'd check the mail, I'd walk back."

"Except it wasn't so nice the last time you did it," he concluded.

"I don't want it to be the last time," she said stubbornly. "I don't want to let him destroy those memories," she said, a wistful note creeping into her voice. She cleared her throat. "And then after… I liked who I was becoming," she admitted. "Me, on my own. Without anyone to tell me what I should do or how I should act. And without a bottle of wine as a crutch."

"I get you," he said quietly.

She tilted her head and looked up at him from the corner of her eye. "Do you?"

"Yes."

"I won't let him take it from me," she said, the steel of determination sharping her tone again. "Either you can walk with me or wait here until I get back."

"I'll walk with you," he answered without hesitation. "Let me tell Deputy Warren it's us coming down the drive. He was a little too excited about a 'stakeout' for my comfort," he said with a smirk.

"Okay. Yeah," she said with a nod. The young deputy on duty had been disconcertingly enthusiastic. "Good thinking."

He called the deputy's number as he followed her out the front door and down the steps to the brick driveway. They walked in silence until they rounded the first bend and the bricks gave way to the well-tended gravel lane lined with trees. As they walked, he maneuvered Kayla to the center of the lane, and for once she didn't fight him on it.

"This is a nice walk," he said, tipping his head back as if to admire the canopy the trees provided.

She chuckled. "You're freaking out as much as I am, but for different reasons."

He looked over at her. She appeared calm, cool and completely in control. "Are you freaking out?" he asked, genuinely astounded.

"Of course I am," she scoffed. "The last time I took this walk, I got shot."

"True." They continued in silence until a strange thought slotted into place and he let loose with a chuckle.

"What's so funny?" she asked as they navigated the next graceful curve in the drive.

"I'm freaking out because the last time you took this walk you got shot, so I guess we're both freaking out for the same reason."

Kayla gave her head a rueful shake as she paused to pick up a bright red maple leaf. Twirling the stem between her fingers, she shot him a sidelong glance. "Is this your way of saying we have a lot in common?"

"It was an observation, but yeah, I guess in this case we do." He paused for a moment to let the thought sink in. Feeling suddenly exposed, he deflected by cracking a joke. "Which is nice, considering you and Whitney have already declared your unending love for me," he added with a playful nudge of his elbow.

"I was thinking about the movie, not the song," she grumbled, ducking her head to hide her smile.

They trudged along, the soles of their shoes crunching the gravel underfoot and occasionally sending a few rocks skittering along the surface. Ryan caught a glint of sunlight reflecting through the trees and drew to an abrupt halt.

Kayla stopped on a dime. "What?"

"Reflection over there," he whispered, motioning to his left.

She squinted in the direction he'd indicated, then a moment later exhaled loudly through her mouth. "I think it's Deputy Warren's car," she informed him. "The drive does a little switchback not far from the gate, remember?"

"Right." The moment she said it, he knew in his gut she was correct. He let the breath he'd been holding seep silently from barely parted lips. After all, someone had to play it cool out here.

Sure enough, they came around the next corner and found the young deputy lounging against the side of his vehicle. "Afternoon, sir. Ma'am," he said, touching the brim of his hat as he straightened away from the car.

"Hello, Deputy," Kayla replied, her voice warm. "Are you okay out here? I asked our caretaker to put a minifridge in the guardhouse. Did you find drinks and snacks in there?"

"Oh, yes, ma'am. Thank you, ma'am," he said, a flush coloring his barely stubbled cheeks.

Ryan refrained from rolling his eyes. "Mrs. Powers wants to check the mailbox."

The young man nodded and hurried to the control panel to open the gate. "I saw the delivery truck go by about thirty minutes ago. If there's something you're waiting on, ma'am, I can check the box for you and call up to the house," he offered.

"You are kind," Kayla said smoothly, "but no. I like the exercise."

Deputy Warren nodded, then stepped back and he and Kayla walked around the gate to the metal box set into the stone pillar.

Sure enough, the box held little more than a bundle of bulk-mail advertisements, postcard reminders and a few standard business-size envelopes. "Hey, look, I'm preapproved for a home-equity loan," she said, waving the envelopes at Ryan.

"Congratulations," he said dryly.

Kayla laughed and flashed another winning smile at the young deputy as they passed. "You call up to the house if there's anything y'all need out here, okay?"

"Yes, ma'am. Thank you, ma'am," Deputy Warren replied eagerly.

Anxious to be away from the road, Ryan hustled her back the way they came. "You can't smile at the young ones like that," he said under his breath. "It scrambles a guy's brain."

"What?" she answered distractedly, a crease appearing between her eyebrows and her steps slowing as she gazed down at an envelope.

Ryan had taken three full steps before he realized

she'd slowed to a halt. Turning back, he closed the distance between them. "What is it?"

"It's from P, P and W," she murmured, tracing a fingertip over the return address, then letting it trail down to the place where her late husband's name was printed in bold black ink. She wet her lips, then offered it up for his examination.

It was all Ryan could do to keep from snatching it from her hand. "Why would they—"

"Mailing list," she answered, cutting him off. She shuffled the envelopes until another piece of PP&W stationary appeared. She was the addressee on this piece of correspondence.

"Mrs. Ayers probably forgot to fix her list," she murmured, almost to herself.

"Fix her list?"

"Nancy Ayers keeps a database. All official firm correspondence is copied to Tyrone at both the house in Bentonville and here. Bill gets copies sent to DC and his place here. Anthony Walton is copied, too, even though, as a judge, he has removed himself from the day-to-day running of the firm."

They walked back to the house in silence, Ryan riffling the pages of the flyers while Kayla turned the envelopes around and around in her hands. The moment they reached the front door, Kayla stopped and took a deep breath. "I'm probably being ridiculous. These are probably nothing but copies of some financial statements or something."

She tore into the envelope addressed to Tyrone and extracted a single sheet with engraved letterhead. Printed in the center of the page in standard twelve-point Courier font was a blunt message.

```
YOU SHOULDN'T HAVE BETRAYED THE
FAMILY.
```

Ryan peered over her shoulder, then snatched the envelopes from her trembling hands. "In. Get inside. Now."

"It wasn't addressed to me," she said in a bewildered tone.

Ryan dropped the mail onto the foyer floor in his haste to lock the doors and rearm the alarm system. He heard the rip of heavy paper behind him, and his heart plummeted into his stomach. He turned in time to see the envelope addressed to Kayla flutter to the floor.

There must not have been much of a message for her, either, because barely a second passed before she thrust the sheet of expensive paper into his stomach, crumpling it at the edges. But rather than admonishments about loyalty, the message sent to Kayla was much more succinct. The page had only two words printed on it.

```
WELCOME HOME.
```

Chapter Eleven

They fought about the messages all day.

Of course, Ryan wanted to leave right away, but she dug in. They were playing a game with her. One with rules she wasn't privy to, but a game, nonetheless. The timing and delivery of the messages didn't make any sense. Whoever it was, intended her to receive the letter addressed to Tyrone. Neither envelope was stamped or postmarked, which meant they'd been hand-delivered after he'd been killed. And after she'd been shot.

Kayla stubbornly refused to go.

Instead, she'd instructed Michelle and Nancy Ayers to comb through the piles of mail that had accumulated from their Bentonville address to see if anything had been sent there. Sure enough, they found two identical envelopes and messages on PP&W stationary buried in the stacks of statements, information disclosures and other nonessential, but first-class, mail. Michelle handed them over to Ethan, and Kayla carefully placed the duplicates into a plastic storage bag, then escaped to her bedroom to avoid further conflict with Ryan.

They ate dinner separately, each slipping down to the kitchen when the other wasn't around.

A strange, buzzing tension filled the house. Kayla found it disquieting. After all, this was hardly the first time they'd clashed over his plans for her protection. But even after hours of mind-numbing television and an attempt to read a book couldn't hold her attention for more than two pages, she had trouble sleeping.

She had an appointment with an obstetrician in Eureka Springs the following morning. With all that was happening, she'd had little time to concentrate on her pregnancy beyond trying to eat decently, get some exercise and try her best not to be killed.

Scheduling regular prenatal visits in Bentonville, Springdale, Rogers or even Fayetteville without anyone finding out would be next to impossible. Arkansas's northwest corridor might be busy and expanding, but since the towns along the interstate tended to bleed one into another, the region was like a stretched-out small town. Gossip spread faster than mayonnaise on a hot day. All it would take would be one whisper about Ty Powers's widow being pregnant and the speculation would fly.

The tension rode with them into Eureka Springs the next morning. Kayla had to bite the insides of her lips to keep from being the one to break it. She had to stand her ground on staying at the lake house. Her intuition told her it was the right place to be. But how was she supposed to explain the certainty of a gut feeling to a man who lived to make plans?

She assured him she'd booked in using her maiden name, something that earned her an approving nod from

Ryan. The man sat still as a statue in the waiting-room chair, his eyes fixed on the toes of his boots as they waited for the nurse to call her back to be examined. She'd sipped water all the way here in preparation for the ultrasound she'd requested. She'd also hear the baby's heartbeat today. According to the books she'd read, she should already have passed some of these milestones, but nothing about this pregnancy was textbook.

She closed her eyes and said a silent prayer it would end better than it began.

So far she hadn't had morning sickness. At least, nothing too severe. There'd been a couple of times the scent of food she usually loved repelled her, and one morning when she discovered the taste of any fruit-flavored yogurt made her stomach curdle, but for the most part she'd been extremely lucky.

She hoped luck held out.

"Kayla Maitland?"

Kayla rose and murmured, "Back soon."

Ryan hummed an acknowledgment, and she gathered her purse.

She froze when the nurse spoke again. "Mr. Maitland? Would you like to come back, too?"

Kayla's cheeks burned as Ryan continued his study of his footwear, blessedly oblivious to the fact the nurse was speaking to him. "Oh, um, I don't think he…" she stammered, casting an apologetic glance at Ryan as he tuned in and his head popped up.

"What?"

"Would you like to come back as well?" She glanced down at the chart in her hand, then back up at them.

"This is going to be an action-packed visit," she added with a cheerful smile.

"You, uh, you don't—" Kayla began again, but the words fell away when she realized Ryan was rising to his feet.

"Yeah, um, sorry. I was zoning out," he said, flashing a winning smile at the other woman. Glancing down at her, he let the smile stretch until the dimple in his cheek appeared. "Where you go, I go, right?"

Ears aflame and face so hot she was sure it would melt off like something out of a sci-fi movie, Kayla fell into step behind the chattering nurse. Before she knew it, the two of them were in an exam room painted a soft pastel green, and the nurse was asking her to strip down.

Kayla glanced around the minute the door clicked shut behind them, but saw no curtain or privacy screen to hide behind. Picking up the neatly folded gown at the foot of the exam table, she turned to Ryan and asked, "What do you think you're doing?"

"It's better this way. If anyone ever figures out you were here, they will assume I'm with you for a reason," he told her. "If someone you know finds out you're pregnant, you can let them think the baby isn't Ty's. It might be safer for both of you."

She couldn't argue the logic, but the subterfuge annoyed her enough to get her hackles up. "You realize I'm about to get naked and have a gynecological exam right in front of you, don't you?"

She had the pleasure of watching him redden from the collar of his shirt to his hairline. "I did not, no," he admitted gruffly. "I was thinking about…" He trailed off, gesturing to the window and the world beyond it.

"Right," she said grimly. With a huff, she shook out the fabric of the gown. "Well, turn around. And no peeking."

She kept her eyes glued to his back as she hurriedly stripped off the soft cotton dress she was wearing and slipped her arms into the gown, bra and panties still in place. Then, feeling adequately covered, she wriggled her way out of her underwear, and placed it all in a bundled wad on the counter beside the small sink.

Holding the front of the gown closed, she shook out the plain white modesty sheet and hopped onto the end of the exam table. She made certain she was covered from head to toe before she lied back with a huff. "Okay. You can stop staring at the wall."

To his credit, he kept his expression carefully blank. "Sorry, I didn't think this part through."

She nodded, clutching the sheet over her chest. "Yeah. Uh, stay up by my head," she instructed. "Or better yet, take a seat." She jerked her chin toward the chair wedged into the corner of the room. "They're usually good about keeping things covered as they go."

Ryan dropped heavily into the chair. "Sorry. I—"

"I get it," she assured him. "Don't worry, this doesn't automatically sign you up to be my Lamaze partner."

But though she'd hoped to lighten the mood with the joke, the realization she would be going through this pregnancy and marking all her baby's milestones alone blanketed her with a heavy melancholy. She blinked back the threat of tears, then swallowed hard as she stared at the mosaic of pastel painted ceiling tiles above her. Maybe Michelle would be her birth partner? Or maybe she'd ask her mom? Either way, this should be the one and only time Ryan Hastings would be asked to go above and beyond his call of duty.

A sharp knock on the door served more as a warning than a request. Before she could respond, a petite, dark-haired whirlwind blew in.

"How are we doing today?" she asked, beaming first at Kayla, then scanning the room until she spotted Ryan. "I'm Dr. Vargas," she said, offering Kayla a hand to shake. "I understand you're new to the area?"

Kayla nodded, then launched into the cover story she'd been concocting since the day she made the appointment. "Yes. With the stress of moving I didn't know I was pregnant." She gave a self-conscious grimace. "I had a little accident a couple weeks ago, and they treated me in the ER. I realized I was late and asked for a test."

Dr. Vargas nodded then made a note on her chart. "It looks like they ran a test at the hospital?"

"Yes, ma'am," Kayla replied "With getting settled and all, this was the first time I could get in."

Dr. Vargas gave her leg a reassuring squeeze as she moved to the foot of the table. "I understand. Sometimes life sweeps in and carries us away, doesn't it?" She patted the end of the table and tugged the modesty sheet down a few inches. "I need you to scoot down a bit."

Dr. Vargas set the chart aside and carefully raised the stirrups on the exam table. "Quite a surprise for you

too, huh, Dad?" she said to Ryan as she set about getting things arranged to her liking.

To his credit, Ryan didn't hesitate long before answering. "Yeah, you could say so."

"Well, you're here now." She grinned at Kayla again.
"You're young and your vitals all appear to be good,"
the doctor said, dividing her attention between the two
of them. "Nothing in the family history other than what
you noted on the intake paperwork?"

Kayla shook her head. "No. I'm healthy as a horse."

"Good to hear." The doctor rolled the stool closer to
the edge of table then helped Kayla position her heels
in the stirrups. "A quick peek under the hood to make
sure everything looks okay, then you're getting a twofer.
We're going to hook you up to a couple machines—
you'll get to hear the baby's heartbeat today and we'll
do your first ultrasound." She beamed at Kayla over the
tented edge of the sheet. "Most moms have to spread
these trips out."

Kayla laughed. "I guess it pays to be oblivious."

"Sometimes it does," the doctor agreed.

She was true to her word and the examination was
quick. As she stripped off her sterile gloves, she assured them everything looked good and seemed to be
on track. She discussed possible dates of conception
with Kayla and then confirmed what the doctor in the
ER doctor had guessed about her progress.

"I'd say you're about at the halfway mark, so you
could be holding your new little sweetheart right around
Valentine's Day."

"Valentine's Day?" Ryan croaked, breaking his silence. "In February?"

"That's when it usually falls," Dr. Vargas said cheerfully. "Better plan on buying twice as many roses, Dad."

"I'm already nineteen or twenty weeks along?" Kayla confirmed, doing the calculations in her head.

"Yep." Dr. Vargas gave her a reassuring smile. "You're one of the lucky ones. You skipped all the pukey stuff at the start. Hopefully, you'll sail right through the rest." She made a note on her chart. "We'll set you up for regular visits every four weeks for now. We'll get down to every week once we're in the home stretch."

"Okay," Kayla responded with a nod. "Thank you."

"No need to thank me. I have the easy job," the doctor replied. "In the meantime, relax, sleep, eat well, get some exercise. Keep things as low-stress as you possibly can, and you'll barely need me at all until the big day."

"Low stress," Kayla said with a laugh.

"I know," Dr. Vargas, said with a winsome smile. "We can always dream, right?"

"Right."

"Okay. Our technician, Stacy, will be in shortly. She'll get you hooked up and we'll take baby's first pictures," she said as she slid her pen into the pocket of her white coat. "Any questions for me?"

Kayla shook her head. "No. I think I'm good."

Dr. Vargas looked over at Ryan. "Dad? You good, too?"

"Good." His voice cracked on the single word, and he cleared his throat. "All good. Thank you."

They were quiet on the ride back to the lake house. Kayla didn't want to talk. She didn't want the radio.

She didn't want to hear anything but the technician's confirmation over and over again.

It looks like you're having a boy.

She held her breath as the gate at the foot of the drive swung inward. Deputy Warren had been replaced by an equally fresh-faced recruit named Bennett this morning. She and Ryan waved simultaneously as they passed, but neither broke the silence. Gravel crunched under the tires as they wound up the drive. It transitioned to the rumble of bricks as they approached the house. Unwittingly, she scanned the front of the house for any sign of intrusion as the SUV crept past the main entrance, then around the side to the garage.

Sunshine bounced off the glasslike surface of the lake. Kayla stared out the passenger window, making no move to open the door even after Ryan killed the engine.

When Ryan spoke, his voice was as rough as the gravel they'd driven over. "Congratulations, Kayla. I'm happy for you."

"Thank you," she responded, unable to tear her gaze from the water. "A boy," she whispered, saying the words aloud for the first time since repeating them back to Stacy for confirmation. She glanced over at Ryan, feeling awkward and exposed in a way she hadn't felt when she was lying on the exam table. "Sorry. Still processing."

"It's a lot."

"Yeah. It is," she said, not bothering to mask the emotion thickening her voice.

She'd cried the entire time they printed out the remarkably clear ultrasound screenshots. Apparently, tears were not an unusual reaction because Stacy hadn't been fazed by them in the least. What she hadn't expected was to look up and find Ryan standing beside the table, his gaze locked on the monitors.

"Would you like to go for a walk?" he asked, nodding to the lakefront. "Some fresh air might do you good."

She laughed at his suggestion. "Aren't you the guy who's always trying to make me stay inside?"

"One-time offer," he said, all stern solemnity.

She smiled at him, blinking back tears she couldn't explain. "I'll take it."

Ryan was out of the car and at the passenger door before she could gather herself. Walking companionably side by side, they skirted the side of the house and cut across the patio. Kayla dropped her purse on one of the chairs, but carried the small clutch of ultrasound printouts with her as they started down the path to the dock. She knew eventually, she'd tack one to a fridge with a magnet and walk past it without ever seeing it again, but for today, she wanted to look her fill.

Ryan shoved his hands into his pockets as they walked out to the end of the swim dock. She didn't miss the way he scanned the shoreline at regular intervals, but she couldn't worry about that now. Now, all she wanted to do was drink in big, greedy gulps of crisp, clear air and hug her baby's first pictures to her chest.

A boy. She was having a boy.

"Will you name him Tyrone?" Ryan asked, giving voice to the question she hadn't allowed herself to ponder.

"I don't know," she answered honestly. "I've thought about it, and I probably should." She turned to him, her nose wrinkling, and confessed, "But I don't want to, though. Is that bad?"

He shrugged. "I can't blame you. It hasn't been the luckiest name to pin on a kid."

She huffed a laugh. "Nope. And you can bet Delray is out of the question," she added.

Ryan looked over at her, his face a mask of seriousness. "He'll thank you one day."

This time, she laughed out loud. "No doubt." She turned, gesturing for him to follow her. "Did you know Ty's dad named his boat the *Stingray*?" she asked.

Behind her, Ryan snorted. "No." She led him back up to the shore, then pointed to a beautifully restored and maintained sailboat, its glossy wooden hull glinting in the sunlight. "There she is. It's a giant pain to take out, but Ty liked to run it around every once in a while. Boat nerds flock to any dock where she's moored."

"No doubt. It looks to be a beautiful boat." He followed her as she made her way along the shore to the boathouse. "I assume the red one is Trey's. I saw photos in the files."

Kayla nodded. "I would have thought it would be impounded, but no doubt Ty made some calls," she said, her tone dry and tinged with disapproval.

"I'm assuming the crime lab got all they could from it," he answered diplomatically.

"Ty was nearly apoplectic," she said softly. "There was no way they were keeping anything that belonged to his precious Trey." The moment the words were out of her mouth, she regretted them. "Sorry. That was inappropriate. Ty was a good father. Maybe a little blind to his son's faults, but I think most parents are."

"Probably," Ryan agreed easily.

Unspoken questions hung in the air between them as they approached the boat slips. Kayla was about to tell him to spit them out so they could get it all over with once and for all, but then she noticed something amiss.

The door to the boathouse, where they stored life jackets, fishing and other water sport accessories, was wide open. One side of the thick hasp had been pried from the bolts securing it to the cedar-shake siding. The other clung to the door, its padlock rendered useless.

"Someone broke into the boathouse," she said, throwing her arm out instinctively to block Ryan's progress.

He grasped her arm, but rather than pushing past her to investigate, he swung her around and hustled up the sloping lawn to the terraced patio. Before she knew it, they were safe inside the house, and Ryan had his phone in hand.

"Reset the alarm. I'm calling the sheriff. Someone must have come around by boat."

Kayla picked up the remote for the smart system and spoke a few commands into the receiver. A second later, the computer-generated assistant assured her the system was fully armed.

Barely a minute passed before they heard the squeak of brakes out front. Ryan took off for the foyer and she followed hot on his heels. Deputy Bennett pulled up in front of the house and Ryan swore softly under his breath. "Go wait in Ty's office," he ordered as he disarmed the alarm. "Remember to lock yourself in."

Kayla watched as he headed out to speak to the young deputy, clearly displeased he'd left his post. When Ryan mapped out the additions he wanted made for the sake of security he had insisted she had a safe room. As one of the few rooms with no exterior access, Ty's office made sense. Still, she had no intention of locking herself in there every time Sergeant Bossy issued an order.

She waited in the foyer, watching Ryan speak to the younger officer through the paned sidelights. She could see the reluctance in the deputy's movements as he climbed back into his cruiser, but Ryan had clearly issued an order for him to return to his post at the gate. She backed up a few steps as Ryan came back inside.

The moment the door closed behind him she ordered the alarm to reactivate.

"You're supposed to be in Ty's office," he reminded her sternly.

"I could see you from where I was standing."

"Which means anyone who was out there could see you, too," he argued. He ran a hand over his face, then shook off his frustration. "If you won't do it for yourself, Kayla, you could at least do it for the baby," he said, gesturing to the pictures she clutched in her hand.

"I don't need you to tell me what I should do for my baby. I'll go in the office and stretch out on the couch, but I won't be locked down."

"We had an agreement—" he began.

"I agreed you could turn the office into a safe room. I never agreed to lock myself in it," she countered.

"Lawyers," he growled.

"Know-it-all cops who don't know a darn thing," she stormed.

"Then tell me, Kayla. Tell me what I don't know so I can do my job better," he challenged.

She sighed, all the fight going out of her. She was

tired of butting heads with Ryan. He was right. He was only trying to do his job. She inhaled deeply, then blew out a breath.

"Okay, fine." She looked him straight in the eye. "Before the sheriff gets here and you make a big deal out of this being Del, I need to tell you people break into the boathouse all the time," she said calmly.

"What?"

"I admit, it freaked me out a little, given the situation, but it's not uncommon. We're in an isolated area. People around here know the place is unoccupied most of the time. We've had boating gear, fishing tackle and all sorts of skis, tubes and boards stolen out of this boathouse."

"How often?"

"Probably a half-dozen times since Ty and I got married, so multiply out over however many years," she said with a wave of her hand.

She lifted her chin a notch. "Now I'm going to go lie down for a bit to keep things low-stress, as per doctor's orders. I trust you can handle things with the sheriff now that you know."

Chapter Twelve

Kayla was right, and it didn't make him happy. According to the Carroll County sheriff's deputies who responded to the call, vandalism and theft from lakeside storage buildings was a common occurrence. But knowing was no comfort.

The storeroom hadn't simply been ransacked by a thief looking for the good stuff. It looked like a tornado had ripped through it. Boating gear and sporting equipment had been tossed around with the kind of random ferocity meant to create mayhem and not to procure merchandise.

After the deputies finished taking their notes and photos, they assured him they would confer with the Powers family's caretaker to determine if anything of value had been taken. After waving them off in the driveway, he placed a call to the sheriff himself, who repeated much of the same information his deputies had imparted. After receiving his assurances of continued vigilance and support, Ryan hung up with an exhausted sigh.

He trudged back into the house and reset the alarm via the keypad rather than the voice commands he could never remember, then made his way to what was Tyrone Powers's home office. There, he found Kayla cozied up on the leather sofa under a chunky knit throw reading a book.

"You get all your reports filed?" she asked without looking up.

"Yeah." He rubbed the back of his neck, wondering where to begin with her. Being in the exam room with her that morning brought her pregnancy into focus. When he'd heard the *whoosh-whoosh-whoosh* of the baby's heartbeat, the reality of it hit him. Kayla's baby wasn't some vague complication they'd need to work around. This was happening. She was pregnant. He'd had visual confirmation of the small human growing inside her.

Should he ask how she was feeling? Would she want to talk about it? Until she'd mentioned the appointment, she'd barely mentioned the topic, so he wasn't sure if it was fair game or not.

"How are...? Are you...?" he began and stopped.

What he'd witnessed that morning was an intimate moment he'd inserted himself into without her prior consent. It was painfully clear to him they needed to talk about the boundaries of their working relationship, but he didn't have the foggiest idea how to approach the conversation.

He chickened out and settled on something else. "What are you reading?"

She held up the book so he could see it. "A classic— *What to Expect When You're Expecting*," she said with a wan smile.

He nodded, then lowered his hand from his neck and pointed to one of the chairs situated in front of the desk. "May I?"

"Sure." Kayla shifted to sit up straighter, marked her page, then placed the book on the low table in front of the sofa.

He turned the chair to face her, then dropped into it. Only then did he notice she'd marked her place in the book with the sonogram photos. Seeing them gave him the launchpad he needed for his apology.

"Listen, I'm sorry about this morning. I wasn't thinking about anything beyond sticking close to you. I had no business barging my way in there, and—"

Kayla held up a hand to stop him. "No. It's okay. Actually, other than the whole awkward gown-and-sheet conundrum, I was glad to have someone there. Have you there," she amended, meeting his eyes. "I do appreciate what you're trying to do for me, Ryan. And maybe this morning's doctor's visit was the eye-opener we both needed." She drew a shaky breath. "It made it so much more real, didn't it?"

Ryan nodded. "Yeah. Scary real," he added with a smile.

She tipped her head to the side. "I keep circling back to the name thing," she told him. He must have frowned because she waved a hand dismissively. "Oh, I know I have months to go, but it's in my head." She gave a short, self-effacing laugh. "Maybe because I feel so much of my life is out of my control. Since Ty isn't around, what to name this baby is the one thing on which I get the absolute last word."

"Makes sense."

"What do you think of Tyler?"

"I think it only matters what you think," he countered.

She grinned. "Excellent evasive maneuver."

He inclined his head in acknowledgment. "Thank you."

"I could call him Ty, like his dad, but he wouldn't be the next Tyrone Delray Powers. He's going to be born into a lot of stuff. The last thing I want is to add the weight of a name, you know? I don't want him to grow up feeling like he has to be a lawyer, or a senator, or even take over the family firm."

She covered her stomach with her hand, and for the first time, Ryan noticed the slight curve beneath the thin cotton fabric. Good manners told him he should look away, that he had no business ogling a pregnant woman, much less one who was also someone he was supposed to be protecting. But what he witnessed this morning had crossed so many lines, he didn't know how he'd ever back up enough to regain any level of detachment.

Uncertain what his role was supposed to be in this conversation, he simply nodded and said, "It sounds like you have been giving it a lot of thought."

"I have. It's all I've thought about since I found out. How do I protect all this for him? Can I keep his birthright intact, but not thrust a whole passel of expectations on him? How do I help him understand the privilege he'll be born into is a blessing and a responsibility, but not a predetermined path?"

Curious, he asked, "Did your husband feel like he didn't have any choice in becoming a lawyer?"

Kayla laughed. "Oh. He didn't. His father made sure both Ty and Bill knew they had to toe the line. Tied things up in trusts. I'm told his will had so many codicils and contingencies it took them days to parse it out." She shook her head. "Another reason why Tyrone wanted to rewrite his will. Apparently, the old one was only slightly less convoluted than his father's, mainly because the trusts and such had already been worked out. Tyrone wanted something simpler. Cleaner. One allowing for more...options."

"Wasn't Trey supposed to take over the firm?"

She nodded. "Yes, but Tyrone didn't stipulate anything beyond immediate succession. If Trey were alive, he could have dissolved the partnership."

"And now you can," he concluded.

"I can, but I won't." She gave him a wan smile. "I talk a good game about not wanting to put too much on him, but it is his legacy." She dipped her chin to her chest, then plucked at one of the thick strands of yarn. "Once this madness is all over, I'll do my best to hold it all together in case he wants it."

"I have no doubt you'll do more than hold it together," he assured her.

"Anyway," she said, swinging her legs down, and turning to face him. "What did the people from the sheriff's department say?"

He gave her a lopsided smile. "They said it happens all the time."

She nodded. "I called Mr. Johnson. He takes care of

the grounds for us. He said he'd come by later today to sort through the mess and see if anything significant is missing." She paused, then shot him a sly smile. "He probably won't come to the house, so if you see a man who's about seventy and has six hairs on top of his head poking around out there, don't shoot, okay?"

"I'll do my best to refrain," he assured her.

That night, Ryan was lying stretched out on the bed in the guest room, remote pointed at the large wall-mounted television. It was late, and the programming available was unsatisfactory. Kayla had gone off to the main suite of rooms hours earlier, but he couldn't settle. He was too keyed up from the day's activities to relax.

Giving up, he pushed the power button and the screen went black. Swinging his legs over the side of the bed, he sat for a moment debating whether he should go down to the kitchen for a snack or try to find something boring to read. His gaze landed on his abandoned sneakers. Glancing down at his gym shorts and T-shirt, Ryan thought about the home gym on the lower level and was forced to admit to himself he'd let his physical therapy slide over the last few weeks.

Blowing out a resigned breath, he picked up his sneakers and padded down the hall to the staircase. A single lamp in the foyer cast a gentle glow over the shadowed furniture in the open living area. Swiping his thumb across the screen on his phone, he turned on the flashlight and headed down the dark corridor beyond Tyrone Powers's home office.

He flipped the switch inside the door of the workout room and let out a low whistle as he took a good look at the assortment of high-tech equipment inside. In addition to a treadmill and elliptical trainer, there was one of those virtual reality bicycles. The far wall was covered in floor-to-ceiling mirrors. Opposite the wall of mirrors sat a large universal weight system complete with bench and leg presses.

Pulling up his favorite workout playlist, he started the music and adjusted the volume to where it was loud enough to hear, but not enough to carry through the house. He began his workout with an easy five-minute walk on the treadmill to get his blood moving and muscles loose.

Then, to get his heart rate elevated, he allowed himself to take a spin on the fancy bike. The program he had selected was called easy mountain trail, but five minutes into the ride, his shirt clung to his back. Moving to the weights, he stripped off his shirt and used it to mop his face.

He was reaching for the shoulder extension bar when he glanced to the right and saw they even had a station complete with water cooler, towels and what he assumed to be a bottle of disinfectant spray to wipe down the machines.

He thought about the gym in Little Rock where he paid ten dollars per month as a membership fee and chuckled. It was nice to avoid doing his sweating and straining, moaning and groaning in a public forum. He worked his way through his arm routine, then allowed himself a trip to the water cooler before putting in the dreaded reps on his legs. He'd crushed the little paper cone in his hand and dropped it into the wastebasket below the cooler when the entire house lit up like a Roman candle.

Three ear-splitting beeps ripped through the silence, then the voice of the virtual assistant built into the security system boomed from the speakers concealed throughout the house.

"Perimeter alert. Security breach. Sector four. Coordinates one-twenty-eight by ninety-eight."

The next set of beeps had him pressing one hand to an ear and patting his hip in search of his weapon.

"Perimeter alert. Security breach. Sector four. Coordinates one-twenty-eight by ninety-eight."

His gun was upstairs.

"Kayla," he shouted as the alert cycled through to the piercing beeps again. Cursing under his breath, he took off at a run through the brightly lit house. "Kayla!" he shouted as he took the stairs two at a time.

He'd nearly reached the top when she burst from her room with a gleaming golf club cocked like a baseball bat. Ryan drew up short at the sight of her. She had on a set of pajama bottoms printed with coffee cups and a tank top. Her feet were bare, and her hair was mussed from her pillow. He met her gaze and found her eyes wild.

Holding up both hands, he assured her, "It's me."

"You set off the alarm?" she asked in a rush.

He shook his head then grabbed her hand and pulled her with him to his room.

"No, I was in the gym."

In his room, he released his hold on her and crossed to the dresser, where he grabbed his sidearm from the pile of detritus he'd off-loaded earlier in the evening. On his way back through the door, he took her by the hand again. The heavy head of the golf club thumped down the stairs, but she didn't relinquish her hold on her weapon.

"Where are we going?" she asked breathlessly.

"We need to get you to Ty's office. It's the safe room, and we can monitor the cameras from his computer, remember?"

The system-generated voice kept blaring out its alert, and the tension inside him rose with each repetition. When they reached the office, the door was locked.

"It worked," Kayla said in an almost reverent hush. "Fingerprint. Do the fingerprint thing."

Ryan nodded. They'd had biometric technology installed on the door locks to this particular room. When the house went into lockdown, the locks could only be opened by Kayla or him using a fingerprint.

He pressed his index finger to the small glass pane, and the locks disengaged. He ushered Kayla into the room, then closed the door behind him, using a similar screen to reset the locks.

"If you ever have to come in here without me, you have to remember to lock the door behind you," he instructed.

"I will."

"It's not perfect, but at least no one else can lock you in. Always run to this room," he shouted, wincing as the alarm screeched again. "If someone follows you in and tries to trap you here, they can twist those knobs all they want, but the door won't lock unless you use your fingerprint."

"I remember."

"We should have practiced," he muttered as he hurried over to the desk and wiggled the mouse to awaken the massive monitor. "We're going to practice," he vowed under his breath.

With two clicks of the mouse, he had the complete video surveillance displayed. Clicking through the multipaned display for close-ups, he checked every interior room before moving on to view the exterior cameras.

"It looks like we're clear in here. I don't see any movement in the house."

"Good."

"I'm not seeing much outside, either. Look at the key, will you?" he instructed, nodding to the map the security consultant had left out on the desk. "Where is sector A?"

Kayla scanned the sketch of the property. "South side. The woods beyond the garage." She pressed her hands to her ears like a child. "Can I turn it off now?"

"I need the coordinates," he reminded her.

The system cycled through its warning again and this time the disembodied voice and Kayla spoke in unison. "Sector four, coordinates one-twenty-eight by ninety-eight."

"System mute," Ryan commanded before the technology could take up its litany again.

"System muted," the virtual assistant said, but the alarm continued to emit its staccato beeps periodically.

Ryan scanned all the screens but the only movement he saw was the deputy's patrol car skidding to a stop in front of the house. "I'll go meet the deputy," he said, straightening to his full height and snatching his gun from the desktop. "Locking you in. Don't go anywhere until I give you all-clear." He stopped at the door to scan his print, turning to pin her with an I-mean-business glare. "I mean it, Kayla. I need you to stay put while we clear everything. Promise me."

She must have been more shaken than she wanted to let on because she didn't even attempt to argue. "I promise."

The app on his phone lit up with a full-screen image of a Carroll County sheriff's deputy in a rumpled uniform. This one was considerably older than the fresh recruits who'd pulled guard duty on previous shifts.

Lifting the phone to his mouth he said, "Sergeant Ryan Hastings, Arkansas State Police. I am armed."

"Deputy Mickey Sallings," the man replied. "My sidearm is holstered, sir. I have backup on standby."

Ryan confirmed the man was unarmed, then keyed in the code to cut off the alarm. The front door locks disengaged, and he swung the heavy wooden door inward, peering out at the uniformed officer. He had his gun pointed down and away, but his grip was sure and his paranoia running high. If anything went sideways, he could get at least one shot off before the deputy could draw.

"Did you see anything?" he asked without preamble.

The deputy gave a short nod. "Yes, sir. A big, beautiful buck ran into the woods yonder," he said, indicating the area on the south side of the garage. "I'd say between ten and twelve points on those antlers." He pulled a face. "Made me wish I had my rifle."

Ryan could only assume it was the general vicinity of sector four. "The only things we're hunting tonight, Deputy Sallings, are intruders."

"I believe he was big enough to set things off, but I'll cruise around back and check the dock. With this place lit up like Las Vegas, I'm betting anyone looking to cause trouble took off as fast as the buck."

"I'll check the garage and inform Mrs. Powers. Let me know if you find anything on the exterior. If not, let the backup know they can stand down."

The officer's gaze slipped down to Ryan's chest and a smirk twisted his lips. "Will do, sir," the older man said, turning away with a salute.

Ryan frowned at the lumbering figure of the deputy as he headed back to his cruiser, then glanced down at the gun in his hand, wondering what the guy found so amusing about being met at the door with a SIG Sauer.

Then he remembered he was shirtless.

Groaning, he closed the door firmly, then reset the alarm via the master panel in the foyer. He was making his way down the hall to the back of the house, planning to go through the breezeway and into the three-car garage before returning to Kayla. He made it to the garage door before he heard a soft hiss and crackle.

"Did he see anyone out there?" Kayla asked, her voice carrying high and clear through the speakers.

He stopped and looked up, even though he knew he wouldn't find the concealed speaker. Setting his jaw, he wished he'd been paying closer attention while Kayla had been interrogating the security specialist. This system had more bells and whistles than any he'd dealt with before. Between the cameras, the speakers and the omnipotent virtual assistant, he was getting a creeping sensation along his nape. Freezing in his steps, he tried to recall exactly what rooms interior cameras covered.

For all he knew, she was sitting there watching him creep through her house like a prowler. A half-naked prowler, he amended, feeling instantly self-conscious. Looking up at the ceiling with a stern glare he half-hoped she could see, he said, "He thinks a deer may have tripped the perimeter alarm. Saw a large buck running into the woods on the other side of the garage."

"Oh." She exhaled loudly, then gave a little laugh. *"Of course. A deer. A buck, no less. Surprised the deputy didn't try to bag himself a trophy."*

"Believe me, he's wishing he was in a deer stand and not a cruiser."

"Where are you?" she asked, her voice husky with exhaustion.

His shoulders slumped with relief when he realized she couldn't see him after all. "I'm about to check the garage. Check the interior cameras again, and if everything looks clear, head on back to bed. I'll shut everything down."

"I'm not seeing anything on any of the monitors," she reported as he unlocked the door to the garage.

"Okay. I think we're good," he murmured as he peered into the cavernous space.

Tyrone Powers hadn't kept any of the usual junk in his garage. Tools and paint cans were for mere mortals, not the kind of people who had their concrete floors coated with shiny swirls of epoxy, and sleek canister lighting designed to showcase even sleeker vehicles. The sight of her sparkling white luxury SUV parked beside his dusty, state-issued domestic model drew him up short. Even the classic Range Rover that Powers kept on the estate looked better suited to the space.

"Okay. Well, I guess I'll take my nine iron and head back to bed," Kayla said, interrupting his thoughts.

"Driver," he corrected without thought.

"What?"

He shook his head then turned to head back into the house to start taking everything down a few threat levels. "Your club. You grabbed a driver. A nice one, too." He shook his head as he recalled the glint of gold he'd seen on the bulbous head of the club. "You were about to tee off on someone with a custom driver. Looked like a Honma, but I'm no pro."

"Could have been a club sandwich for all I know," she replied. *"Ty always kept this set in his closet."*

He chuckled. "I'm glad you had something close at hand. Tomorrow, we'll talk more about security procedures, but for now, try to get some rest."

"Okay." The sound of a massive yawn swooshed through the speakers and she gave a helpless laugh. *"Sorry."*

"No worries," he said as he headed back into the kitchen area. Glancing out at the spotlit terrace, he spotted Deputy Sallings trudging up the path from the lakefront. "Try to get some sleep. I'll make sure everything is good down here."

"I have no doubt," she answered. *"Good night, Ryan, over and out."*

"Good night, Kayla," he replied. Then, lifting the remote control she'd left on the kitchen counter, he spoke directly into it. "Intercom off. Reset lighting. Set system to standby armed."

The lights dimmed and Ryan flipped the switch on the terrace lighting to signal the deputy to stand down. Blowing out a breath, he looked down at the gun gripped in his right hand. His phone weighed down the left side of his gym shorts. His knee throbbed; a reminder he wasn't quite up to full-on sprints up and down sets of stairs. The sweat from his workout and residual adrenaline cooled on his skin, making him shiver, but he dismissed the notion of heading back to the gym to retrieve his shirt.

It would be there in the morning, he decided as he made his way to the staircase, his feet heavy as blocks of cement. Suddenly, he was so tired he wasn't sure he'd make it upstairs to his room before he collapsed in a heap.

Chapter Thirteen

Despite the late night, Kayla awoke before the sun rose. Pulling a robe she rarely used from the back of her closet, she slid it on over her pajamas and padded from the room. She wasn't going to get any more sleep, no matter how badly she wanted it.

Though she knew there was no sense in worrying about things she'd done prior to discovering she was pregnant, Kayla couldn't help but fret about the copious amounts of coffee and wine she consumed in those early weeks. As if she could undo the damage done, she began guzzling water like she could detoxify in preparation for the new arrival. She knew it didn't make sense, but logic had hightailed it out of her life months ago.

She held tight to the rail on her way down the stairs, and let loose a monstrous yawn as she shuffled into the kitchen. Humming tunelessly, she pulled a pitcher of filtered water from the fridge and carried it over to the island.

Water sloshed over the side of the glass when she first took aim, but soon it was filled to the brim. After setting down the pitcher as if it was a hand weight, she lifted the glass to her lips and began the day's hydration staring out into the predawn haze that hung low over the lake.

The first rosy hints of the coming dawn reminded her of the inspirational poster she'd had in her first apartment after college. It was an ode to ambition and determination, complete with a pithy one-liner she'd thought doubled as a mantra back in the day. After grinding her way through law school, she'd practically wallpapered her fridge door with sayings about living each moment of her life without remorse.

Now, her fridge was a spotless expanse of expensive stainless steel, her life was more exhausting than exhilarating and she toted around a full set of baggage stuffed with regrets. Some big, most small, but every one of them painful in its own way.

She cringed to think of all the times she'd gone to bed in a snit because one of Ty's friends or her old colleagues made a sly remark at her expense. Taking off the day after her fight with Trey at the gala to lick her wounds and drown her sorrows in wine. The short, terse texts were meant to make him feel guilty, but so rarely worked. Refusing to return her husband's one call that fateful Saturday evening. Hoping he wouldn't be home so they wouldn't have to repeat the argument about the way Trey had treated her. Not somehow sensing the man she loved had been killed long before she'd deigned to come home.

The last one stung the most.

Contrary to popular opinion, she had loved Ty. She'd loved him so much that not fitting into his world had nearly destroyed her. And now, because he'd changed his will to reflect her place in his life, someone had killed him.

Del.

Del had killed Ty.

Or maybe he'd hired someone to do it.

For weeks the possibility cycled through her head. No matter what she'd seen, or thought she'd seen when she'd been winged at the mailbox, it was still hard for Kayla to accept Del Powers had been the one to kill Ty and Trey. It was one thing to shoot at someone who bore no relation to you and threatened your livelihood from a distance. Killing the uncle who'd always doted on you and a cousin you'd grown up with at close range… walking into a man's home and shooting him and his son before they even had time to react…

No, those things were something entirely different.

The coroner's report came back indicating no signs of defensive wounds. The scene showed no real sign of struggle. It had to have been a professional hit.

The Del she knew would not be capable of committing a crime so coldhearted.

The mists shifted, casting shifting shadows across the smooth surface of the lake. A tiny ripple cut through the flawless surface like a concealed zipper. It was the barely perceptible wake of a small boat. A canoe? A kayak? A flatboat with a trawling motor? Her eyebrows drew together as she stepped closer to the window, her gaze mapping the trajectory of the track.

Was someone out there? A fisherman? Was it Del?

The wake was subtle. If the morning hadn't been so

still, the water so mirrorlike, she might never have noticed it. About a quarter mile south of the house, the
shoreline protruded into the lake. One of dozens of fin-
gerlike spits of land divided the underpopulated end of
the lake into the coves and inlets fishermen adored.

She blinked to clear her vision. No, she hadn't been
seeing things. Tiny waves were absorbed by the relent-
lessly placid lake, but there was a disturbance taking
place somewhere.

As if on cue, a large bird swooped from a low tree
limb, nearly skimming the surface of the water as it
made its way from one side to the other. She lowered the
glass and forced herself to take a few calming breaths,
all too aware her heart rate had spiked.

"An owl looking for breakfast," she murmured to
herself, curling her hand in until the cool glass pressed
against her throat.

She forced herself to stand there, unflinching. She
and Ryan had been as jumpy as toddlers hyped up on
sugar these past few days. The scare last night had
pushed them both to peak paranoia. It was high time
one or both of them got a grip.

Lifting the glass to her lips with a trembling hand,
she forced herself to gulp the contents. Staring sight-
lessly out at the lake, she drank until she drained the
glass dry, then topped it up again. She was halfway
through guzzling glass number two when a gravelly
male voice nearly made her jump out of her skin.

"You're up early."

She spun around and set down the glass so hard she
was surprised it hadn't shattered on the granite coun-

tertop. Her heart in her throat, she glanced back at the lake, but all hints of the ripple had disappeared.

Drawing a calming breath, she pressed her hand to her hammering heart and focused on the intruder she could see clear as day. "I cannot believe you'd sneak up on me after a night like last night," she accused.

Ryan winced and a flush of red crept up his neck. "Sorry. I thought you might have heard me coming."

She glanced pointedly at his bare feet, then noted with some relief he was wearing a shirt with his plaid pajama bottoms. "I guess you're pretty light on your feet."

He chuckled, then made his way to the single-cup coffee maker. "One thing I've never been accused of being."

"I like to be first," she said, adding a playful little sniff as she lifted her glass of water in a silent toast. "Good morning."

"Morning."

He placed a mug under the spigot and lowered the boom on the coffee pod. In one fluid move, he rolled to his right and stood facing her, his hips propped on the edge of the counter. He crossed his arms over his chest, and she did her best not to fixate on the way the bulge of his biceps pulled the cotton sleeves tight.

She put the glass to her lips and drank as if she needed to put out some internal fire.

Ryan's state of undress the previous night had been beside the point in the moment. As a matter of fact, it hadn't even registered he was shirtless until she was watching him leave Ty's office dressed in gym shorts, sneakers and carrying a sleek black gun. It had taken hours of tossing and turning to put the image out of her mind.

First, there was the fact her personal-protection officer was ripped. Equipped with the rippling muscles she thought only underwear models sported. Then, there was the fact she had not only noticed how built the man was, but the ensuing tsunami of guilt had also engulfed her the moment she'd allowed herself to dwell too hard on it. And finally, the righteous indignation flew in on the heels of guilt. After all, she was a single female swimming in a whole sea of pregnancy-induced hormones. She would have had to have been dead not to notice him.

It wasn't until he tipped his head to the side inquiringly that she realized she'd drank all her water and stood holding an empty glass to her lips as she soaked in the sight of him.

"You doin' okay?" he asked.

She lowered the glass and grabbed the pitcher again. Slopping the rest of the water into the glass, she nodded a shade too vigorously. "Yeah. Fine." She hesitated, then gave in with a wan smile. "Well, obviously not fine. I didn't get much sleep."

"Yeah, me, either." He pushed away from the counter and reached for the now-empty pitcher. "Here, I'll get a refill while my coffee brews."

Her first impulse was to argue, but she relented and allowed him to remove the pitcher from her hand. The busier they were, the better. She didn't need him in her direct line of sight, given her poor impulse control. Her gaze fixed on the water beyond the windows and she stifled a yawn.

"What time was Michelle heading out here?" Ryan asked, his voice still husky.

"I'm pretty sure it'll be sometime this afternoon," Kayla said. "I'm curious to see what it is she'll think she'll find in Tyrone's office. We've gone through most of the files in there, and all of the paperwork in both his home and office safes."

"Did she say which case she was focusing on?"

Kayla shook her head. "No, but I get the feeling it has something to do with Harold Dennis. She said she'd been working with some of the forensic accountants on her team and wanted to dig a little deeper."

Ryan gave a noncommittal hum as he pulled the steaming mug of coffee from beneath the spigot. She watched as he inhaled deeply, his eyelids lowering to half-mast in appreciation before he blew across the surface of the coffee and chanced a quick sip. His wince told her he hadn't been patient enough.

"What's on your agenda for the day?" he asked, setting aside the mug to let it cool.

"Nothing much," she said with a shrug. "I thought I'd get dressed and maybe we could take a walk around. I'm feeling cooped up."

He nodded his bottom lip for a moment then dipped his head assent. "Yeah, I think it might be good for both of us to have some fresh air. Clear the cobwebs."

She offered him a half-smile. "We can go looking for deer tracks."

"Oh, boy," he said, deadpan, and reclaimed the mug.

"Let's give it a little time, though," he suggested. "I have a feeling I'm going to be waking up pretty slow this morning."

Kayla smiled. "I was thinking maybe I'd head back to bed for a couple hours."

He nodded. "Not a bad idea. What do you say we meet back here at about ten?"

Kayla tipped up her glass and drained the last of her water. "Sounds great," she said as she placed the glass in the top rack of the dishwasher. "See you in a little while."

True to their word, they met back in the kitchen, but well before ten o'clock. She'd managed to doze for a couple of hours and felt far more refreshed than she had earlier. Still, the restless night tugged at her energy levels.

The sun was high and bright in the sky when they stepped onto the patio. Ryan carried the voice-activated remote control for the alarm system, clutching it tight in his hand like a talisman.

"Good thing I'm not into jogging," she said dryly. Lifting her arms over her head, she allowed herself a long luxurious stretch. "If you made me go through those security protocols one more time, I might have taken off at a dead run to get away."

"You'd probably succeed. I think my days besting people in foot races are over."

She glanced down at his leg. He'd never tried to hide his limp, but it was clear Ryan didn't particularly want to talk about it. The one time she had asked, he'd simply said it was a severely torn meniscus and left it at that. No further explanation as to the how or what happened.

Feeling emboldened by the previous night's activities, and considerably more friendly toward him than she had been in the beginning, Kayla worked up the nerve to ask him again. "Did you tear up your knee diving in front of a bullet?"

The question startled a laugh from him. "I wish." He gave his head a rueful shake then gestured to the lake. "By land or by sea?"

She consciously didn't mention anything about the small waves she'd seen on the surface of the misty water morning. The last thing she needed was for Ryan to go into full lockdown mode because she was bleary-eyed and letting her imagination get the better of her.

"Let's walk along the shore to the woods then come back around to the garage and the driveway. We'll look to see if the buck left any tracks behind."

"Who knew you'd be so into the wildlife scene?" he teased.

"I'm an Arkansan. This won't be the first time I've gone tromping around behind a deer." As they walked down to the dock, she cast a sidelong glance at him from under her lashes. "I'm not so easily distracted, you know."

He sighed heavily. "You don't know how badly I'd like to tell you I was injured while doing something epic," he said, his tone bone-dry.

"Ooh, the story gets more intriguing. It wasn't heroic?"

"Not in the least." An expectant silence between them. "I got pushed around by a bunch of eighteen-year-olds who were super-stoked about heading to the Big Dance."

She glanced over at him quizzically, trying to sort out what kind of school dance could possibly require the presence of state-police officers. "A dance? Like homecoming? Prom?"

He let out a scornful laugh. "No," he said, wagging his head hard. "The. Big. Dance. The NCAA basketball tournament." Her blank expression must have given her away because he continued. "I was providing security for the university's head basketball coach. A win would give them a spot in the tournament for the first time in years," he explained patiently.

Recognition dawned. "Oh! Big Dance," she said, nodding sagely. "I'm with you now."

"Yeah, so nothing as dramatic as throwing myself in front of an assassin's bullet."

"I'd like to see the person brave enough to take a shot at the first coach to lead our team through its first winning season in years. I'm betting the crowd would have taken them down in two to three seconds flat."

"It took some frat boy about three to take me down," he said wryly. "I had a prime seat on the floor. If you check the footage you can see me clutching my leg as I watched my primary protectee get carried away by a throng of freshman who probably haven't figured out how to work the laundry machines in the dorms yet."

"Yet they took you out," she said dramatically. "I'm starting to get worried." She leaned in to bump her shoulder against his, letting him know she was pulling his injured leg.

"You probably should."

"I'm only kidding. And I am sorry."

He accepted her sympathies with grace, inclining his head, then motioning to the lawn leading to the large garage built out of the same native stone as the house and its extensive terraces. "There are the tracks," he said, pointing to dark impressions in the neatly maintained lawn.

Kayla followed the direction indicated by this index finger, then gave her head a slow shake. "Ty would have been so excited," she said softly. She drew to a halt and looked up at the sky, blinking back the heat of unexpected tears. She could feel a flush prickling her skin, but she was beyond worrying about embarrassing herself with Ryan Hastings. They had been living in close quarters for weeks now. He'd seen her at her best and her worst, and everything in between.

"Was he a hunter?" he asked quietly.

Kayla smiled a little as she tried to determine the correct answer to his question. "He went to deer camp every year, but I think it was more for the socializing than anything else. He liked to be out in the woods, tracking, waiting, watching. He wasn't big on trophy hunting, though."

Ryan nodded. "I pretty much feel the same way. It's nice to get out. Peaceful to sit in the woods and listen to the sounds all around, but I couldn't care less if I ever took a shot or not. But I admit I am a fan of a well-cooked venison steak."

They followed the tracks from where the deer had entered the perimeter not far from the lakefront. It was clear to see the spot where the animal found itself caught up short by the clamor and clangor of the high-tech security system. Recalling the cacophony of noise from the night before, Kayla couldn't blame the poor, frightened creature for turning tail and running for the safety of the woods.

Glancing over at the house, she gestured to the driveway. "Let's walk down to the bottom of the drive again."

"You expecting more mail?" he asked, instantly wary.

She shook her head. "No, but I don't want to be afraid to walk on my own property."

"Deputy Warren was on duty, but he got called out to check an accident. Maybe we should stick close to the house."

"We won't open the gate," she promised. "We'll walk down and back. I need the exercise."

He acquiesced without another word of protest, tactfully failing to mention the well-equipped home gym he'd obviously been using the night before. She didn't ask if he was carrying his gun. She'd once watched her best friend pull a gleaming gun out of a holster she wore beneath a pair of exquisitely tailored suit pants. The quilted vest he'd shrugged on before going out didn't fool her. Ryan Hastings was armed to the teeth.

They continued in companionable silence until the brick pavers gave way to the gravel. "How come they never paved the whole drive?" he asked, their footfalls crunching on the rocks.

She shrugged. "Ty said something about wanting the driveway to be as inconspicuous from the road as possible. But given how ostentatious the house is…" Ryan chuckled as she let the thought trail off. "I can't tell you. I will say from everything I heard from Ty and Bill over the years, Tyrone Senior was a fairly mercurial man. He had a reason for doing things the way he did them, and he didn't appreciate being questioned about his motives."

"The architecture is a bit…eccentric for the area."

"A nice way of putting it," she said with a laugh. They rounded the last bend and the paved road beyond the gate came into view. "It's strange to admit, but as over-the-top as the house is, I feel more at home here than anyplace I've lived since I left my parents' house."

"Maybe because deep down you're over-the-top?" he said, a teasing note in his tone.

"Oh, def—" Before she could get the words out, the stench of rotting fish hit her right in the face.

And the gut.

"Oh!" She covered her mouth with her hand, but it was too late. Stumbling to her left, she hurried to the spot beyond where the deputies had been parking while on duty and tossed her breakfast.

"Stay here," Ryan ordered.

As if she could take off running while she was bent over retching. He came back a minute later, the toes of his shoes wet with dew from their trek across the lawn and now coated with dust from the gravel. She glanced up to find him pulling his shirt up over his mouth and nose, but there was no quelling the rebellion in her abdomen.

"Fish," Ryan confirmed. "Someone probably tossed what was left of their catch out of a car."

She wiped the back of her hand across her mouth but

didn't dare lower it as she inhaled through her mouth. The last thing she wanted to do was trigger another round of retching. "Happens all the..." The words died on her tongue as she raised her head and spotted a shadowy figure melting into the shadows of the woods on the far side of the drive.

Her mouth was dry.

Eyes wide, she could only stare at the spot where the man had stood a moment before.

He was gone, of course.

Gone, but not forgotten.

When her wits returned, all she could do was extend a pointed finger at the spot near the base of a spindly pine as she whispered, "Del."

Chapter Fourteen

He didn't think, he reacted.

But he should have thought. He should have thought of her safety. He should have made certain she was locked down and there was no way Del Powers could get to her. But he didn't do any of those things.

"Go! Get in the gate house," he instructed, propelling her in the direction of the stone outbuilding.

He didn't look back to see if she followed his instructions.

He was too busy responding.

Ryan took off after the shadowy figure like a rookie. He ran headlong into the woods, forgetting his mission. Completely disregarding years of training. Like a greenhorn, he plowed into the underbrush, his weapon drawn and Del Powers's name bellowing from his lungs.

He knew better. But he couldn't stop charging forward.

Branches tore at his arms and underbrush tangled around the legs of his jeans. Scanning the area, he caught sight of a shadow ahead and to his left, heading away from the house. He ran another fifty feet deeper into the woods before his toe caught a tree root.

He went down on his knees. Hard.

The impact sent a jolt of pain radiating through his body. He lost his grip on his gun. The thick mat of pine needles and fallen leaves swallowed the weapon like quicksand. A sick dread twisted his stomach. The fall did something to his already injured knee. Something he knew in his gut was bad. Career-changing bad.

The realization brought him back to his senses.

Scraping around on the ground in search of his weapon, he muttered under his breath, "This is it. You're done. And you should be done. You should be canned for—" He allowed the self-recrimination to trail off as he fingers closed around the stock of his weapon.

A guttural growl ripped from deep inside him as he pushed to his feet.

His knee was toast.

But he couldn't think about the pain now. He had to focus on heading back to the gatehouse.

He'd left his primary unprotected.

A mistake he'd never made before, and one he'd never have the opportunity to make again. Which would be a good thing. Because if he was enough of a fool to go tearing off into the woods chasing shadows while the person he was protecting cowered in an unsecured outbuilding, he deserved to be handed a radar gun and busted down to patrol.

Limping, he made his way back to her, making deals with whatever higher power that might be listening the entire way.

If something happened to Kayla or her baby, he'd never forgive himself.

He checked over his shoulder every few steps. At

the edge of the trees, he paused to catch his breath and check the area. He cursed himself for acting like a wounded wildebeest trying to make his way from the watering hole back to safety without a lion spotting him.

From this vantage point, he could see the stringer of gutted fish tied to the wrought-iron gate. Someone had left them a calling card.

And he'd left Kayla alone.

"Kayla," he grunted as he pushed away from the tree trunk and hobbled his way across the gravel drive toward the gatehouse.

The woman in question came out of the woods from the opposite direction. "Here. Sorry." She waved her hand in front of her face. She stopped in her tracks and frowned as she watched him approach. "You're hurt. Did Del—"

"I fell," he admitted through gritted teeth. "No one to blame but myself."

She hurried to his side, slipping up under his arm as if she could support him. Ryan appreciated the thought, but at the moment his pride was throbbing about as insistently as his knee, and he was angry at the world.

"I told you to stay in the gatehouse," he snarled.

She scowled at him when he shook off her attempt to drape his arm over her shoulders. "I had to get upwind. Let me help you."

"If I try to lean on you, I'm more likely to topple us both over," he groaned. "Don't worry about me. We have to get to the house."

"Did you see him?" she asked, sounding breathless as she kept pace with his determined clip.

"I saw something. Not sure if it was him, or our friend the buck," he admitted. "Are you sure you saw Powers?"

She paused long enough for him to glance over at her. At last, she shook her head. "I'm not sure of anything these days. For all I know, it wasn't even Del who shot me. I don't know."

Her insecurity proved to be as difficult for him to handle as his own. "Don't. Don't start doubting yourself now. If your gut says you saw him, you need to trust your intuition."

Sage advice from a man whose own instincts had him chasing off into the woods rather than doing his duty by her.

"Do you think you reinjured your knee?" she asked quietly.

The driveway sloped downhill toward the waterfront, which made controlling his momentum breathtakingly painful. The trek back to the house seemed ten times as long as the walk to the gate. He was winded, sweating and, much to his consternation, leaning heavily on Kayla by the time they reached the house. He managed to pull the security-system remote from his pocket and disarmed the alarm.

"Who should I call about your leg?" she asked as she deposited him on the large sectional sofa in the open-plan living area.

"Set the alarm," he instructed from between clenched teeth.

Without much finesse, he tossed the system remote in her direction. It clattered to the floor at Kayla's feet.

Not bothering to ask permission, he swung both legs onto the sofa with a harrumph of agony, then fell back against the cushions, flinging an arm over his eyes.

He was too wiped out to even pretend he could tough it out.

Dimly, he registered the computer-assisted confirmation that the system was armed. Kayla sat on the edge of the large, square coffee table right in front of him. He could feel her stare but couldn't bring himself to meet it.

"Ryan? What can I do to help?" she asked gently. "Do we need to go to the emergency room?"

He shook his head as he lowered his arm, but kept his eyes screwed shut against the double whammy of pain and humiliation. "No. No need."

There would certainly be another surgery in his future. Months on crutches. Endless sessions of physical therapy. But for now, the best anyone could prescribe for him would be rest, ice and painkillers. He asked for the most palatable of those three.

"Do you have an ice pack?"

She bobbed her head. "Ty's back would go out on him every once in a while. I think there's one in the freezer."

Without being asked, she grabbed a throw pillow from one of the oversized armchairs. "Lift," she commanded. He did as he was told, biting the inside of his lips as she placed the pillow under his leg. "Do you have anything you can take?"

He thought of the bottle of pills in the bottom of his shaving kit but shook his head. He was not willing to take a narcotic while he was responsible for her safety and well-being. Plus, she'd recently completed a stint in rehab. Though he was pretty sure that pills were not a problem for her, he didn't want to be the one to tempt her. Particularly after his hubris had left her vulnerable.

"I can take a couple over-the-counter anti-inflammatory tablets, if you have some handy."

"We do," she said with a brisk nod. "Be right back."

He wanted to let her go without asking for anything more, but to do so would only protect his ego.

"And Kayla?" he called before she could get away entirely.

"Yeah?"

"Better call Ethan. Tell him you're going to need someone else up here with you," he said gruffly.

"Someone else?"

He allowed his eyes to drift shut even as he heard her coming close again.

"What do you mean get someone else?" she demanded. "Are you quitting?"

He grimaced, then opened his eyes to find her glowering down at him, her hands on her hips.

"No, I'm not quitting," he replied, letting his disgust at the notion seep into the words. "But I'm not any good to you like this." He waved a hand at his knee, where the pain throbbed in time with his pulse.

"You're quitting," she concluded.

"It's not about me or my commitment to the job. I'm getting you someone who can literally chase down the bad guy, Kayla."

"I'll get a German shepherd," she said as if a dog was the obvious answer to all her problems.

"Kayla—"

"Ryan," she countered.

He sighed, then leveled his best cop stare on her. The woman didn't flinch. "You need someone who isn't banged up."

"You're my protection agent," she announced. "Bring in anyone else you think might be helpful, but you're stuck with me."

"You didn't even want protection," he argued.

"I've gotten used to you," she replied without missing a beat.

"You fight every plan I try to put in place."

"I'm a lawyer. We're trained to argue."

"I'm a liability to you now," he pointed out.

"You are one of the handful of people I trust most in this world," she said plainly.

He sighed and closed his eyes. "Fine. Tell Michelle to bring Ethan with her. If I'm sticking around, we need to talk out next steps, and you are going to have to agree to go along with the plan." He pointed at her, his expression stern. "You got me? No arguments, no pushback."

She hesitated only a moment before nodding. While she went to hunt down the ice and analgesics, he almost convinced himself the hesitation was a good thing. If she'd agreed too readily, he would have been suspicious. Then again, the fact she'd agreed at all made his scalp prickle. If the sensation hadn't felt so darn good in contrast to the pain pulsating in his leg, he might have stopped to question her too-easy acquiescence.

He was still on the sofa with his leg propped up when Michelle and Ethan arrived. They came bearing another freezable ice pack, along with a box of small single-use packs he could employ between more serious rounds of chilling.

Ryan knew he must have looked as wretched as he felt when Ethan failed to greet him with the expected razzing an agent was usually subjected to following an on-the-job mishap.

"Hey, man," Ethan said as he took a seat in the chair adjacent to the sofa. "How bad do you think it is?" he asked in a low voice as Michelle followed Kayla into the kitchen to see to the ice-pack rotation. "Game-ending? Season?"

The guys they came up through the ranks with often referred to the stages of career denouement using sports analogies. When he wasn't the one who was laid up, shifting the dialogue from medical jargon to athletics seemed to make conversations easier. Now he realized the lightheartedness of those conversations had been entirely one-sided.

Meeting Ethan's gaze, he said, "Career-ending."

"Nah," Ethan said with a dismissive shake of his head. "I mean, I know it's bad, but another few months of desk duty and you'll be on your feet again."

"Maybe," Ryan said, but his tone was dubious. "But even if I am, I can't do the kind of work I have been doing."

"You can always switch lanes," Ethan interjected.

But Ryan was already shaking his head. "The only place for me to go is behind a desk, and the thought of being glued to an office chair for the rest of my days…" He let the thought trail off and gave a visible shudder. "Nope. Not for me. I could do it for a while when I thought I'd be back at it again, but to be sent from the dugout to the front office is too depressing to even think about."

"There are other options," Ethan argued.

"Not ones I would want," Ryan said, shooting his friend a pointed glance. "Listen, I know you don't mind spending your days kicking over rocks to see if anything slithers out, but I like to be in the thick of things, you know?"

"You like to run with the big dogs," Ethan teased.

"I'd like to be able to run at all," Ryan said morosely. "But, yeah. I like what I do, and there's no way for me to keep doing it with a bum knee."

"Maybe, maybe not," Ethan said, glancing up as Michelle and Kayla reappeared with one of the instant packs. "You don't have to decide anything today."

"Decide anything about what?" Kayla asked.

"About where to go next," he said, meeting her stare directly.

"Go? I'm not going anywhere," Kayla insisted.

Before he could open his mouth to retort, Michelle jumped into the fray.

"Before we get into all that, I need to tell you what we've discovered in the case against Harold Dennis."

Ryan and Kayla glowered at one another for a moment longer. But Ryan couldn't miss the look of puzzled annoyance on Kayla's face as her natural curiosity got the better of her.

He was glad for the reprieve. He needed more time to build his case in his head.

"What about Harold Dennis?" he asked, hoping whatever tale Michelle had to spin would be a lengthy one.

Michelle took a seat on the arm of the chair where Ethan had settled himself then waited until Kayla set in the chair opposite before beginning her story.

"Okay, so you know we suspect Harold Dennis was funneling money through his client, DevCo. The company itself is nothing more than a shell corporation he was using to launder money for a real-estate-investment scheme among other streams of income." She paused long enough to give each of them a chance to nod or murmur affirmations they were all up to speed.

"You know the tricky thing with laundering cases is they're often shell corporations within shell corporations within shell corporations… It's basically the three-card monte game played out in legal paperwork."

"Sometimes it can be nearly impossible to find where it all started," Ethan agreed with a nod.

"Yes, it can. Anyway, we've had some of our best IT people wading back through the lineup of entities, trying to find the origin story. Since no one's talking, it's up to us to sort through the data we've acquired and make sense of it."

Ryan snorted. "Which means you're basically wading through data up to your armpits," he interjected.

Michelle gave him a rueful smile. "Feels like it."

"Did you catch a break?" Kayla asked, cutting to the chase.

Michelle shot her an exasperated look. She seemed miffed by the notion of anyone wanting to cut out the elaborate buildup of months and months of painstaking research and investigation. Ryan couldn't blame her. Then again, Kayla was a lawyer, not a cop. She didn't appreciate the unraveling of the story the way the rest of them did. She only wanted to know the facts so the attorney in her could poke holes in them.

"We believe the development firm at the start of this whole thing was called DelCo, rather than DevCo," Michelle answered, a small smug smile tipping the corners of her mouth upward.

"DelCo?" Kayla repeated.

Michelle smile grew even more smug as it stretched. "Interesting, isn't it?"

Kayla hummed noncommittally. "I don't suppose he was kind enough to list himself as the principal when he filed articles of incorporation."

Michelle shook her head, but her Mona Lisa smile stretched into a grin a mile wide. "Well, no. Not his name," she answered, her tone coy.

"Oh, my God." Kayla threw her hands up in exasperation. "Fine, yes, you've done a wonderful job digging this all out. You're amazing. Mindblowing. Now tell me whose name was on the paperwork and what you think this all means," she demanded.

To her credit, Michelle refused to let Kayla's impatience rain on her parade.

"DelCo was a small real-estate holding consisting of three area mobile-home parks. They were purchased as an investment holding by William Powers, on the occasion of his eldest son, Delray's, eighteenth birthday."

"Good enough for me," Ryan announced.

Turning his gaze directly on Kayla, he said, "These people are all tied up in each other, and you are the one standing in their way. You are the one throwing the wrench into them getting what they want. They are not going to be satisfied until you are—" he paused "—neutralized."

A startled laugh burst from her. "Neutralized," she repeated, holding his gaze. Then, she rolled her eyes and turned her attention back to Michelle. "You're telling us you can pretty much tie the three of them up tightly on the financial malfeasance," she concluded.

"Given the activities they ran through DevCo's accounts, I can say with a strong degree of certainty each of the parties were aware the money moving through the company, and by proxy, through the firm. From what we can trace, a good portion of it went into Harold Dennis's personal accounts, as well as accounts owned by William and Del Powers. A significant amount found its way into Senator Powers's Powers for the People campaign coffers as well."

"If they know you know all this, why keep stonewalling?" Kayla asked. "Why not cooperate in exchange for leniency?"

"Because they've gone too far," Ethan responded, his tone grave.

"From what we can tell, they did their best to keep this client's transactions off Tyrone's radar. But, of course, someone got greedy," Michelle said, making a helpless gesture to the inevitability.

"Someone? Singular?" Kayla persisted.

Michelle shook her head. "It appears all three of them were using DevCo for their own purposes, but I don't know at this point if any of them were aware of how deep the others might be playing."

"You think they were all dipping into the money?" she asked.

But, in an instant, Ryan realized they weren't asking the right question. It popped into his head like a flashing neon sign. And the answer might be the key to unlocking this mystery and so many more.

"Where was the money coming from?" he asked gruffly.

"Various sources," Michelle replied. "One of the more lucrative was some sort of time-share investment scam." She made a face of utter distaste. "From what we can tell it was marketed primarily to retirees moving down from up north."

"Snowbirds," Kayla murmured.

Ryan nodded. Arkansas saw more than its share of seniors looking to escape harsh northern winters while still enjoying a full four-season cycle.

"Exactly," Michelle said. "They stayed low-rent as far as income properties. Mobile homes, small apartment complexes, a few single-family dwellings in neighborhoods. Coincidentally—or not—most of the properties are in areas that have become eligible for public-housing vouchers since Senator Powers took office."

"You're telling me they were triple-dipping senior citizens, people who are economically disadvantaged, and the federal government?" Kayla asked.

The two women locked gazes and Michelle issued a clarification. "Federal and state governments."

"Those are some pretty high stakes," Ryan observed. He fixed his attention on Kayla, watching her absorb the information.

Michelle said softly, "You said your husband was suspicious of the company as a client, and of Harold's handling of the account."

"Yes. He saw there was a higher than customary rate of investment exchange, and startlingly high billable hours being spent on a client that until a few years ago had been reasonably insignificant to the bottom line at P, P and W."

"Do you think he suspected his brother's involvement?" Ethan asked.

Ryan watched Kayla closely as she turned over the possibility in her mind. In the end, she sighed and shook her head. "No. I don't think he believed Bill was involved in anything suspicious."

"Do you think he might have suspected Del?" Michelle persisted.

Again, Kayla shook her head. "He only said something to me about Harold. Not surprising. Bill and Del are family, and while Hal may have been something like family, there was no actual blood connection."

She sighed heavily, and Ryan saw her slip a protective hand over her abdomen.

"Family was the unbreakable bond to Tyrone. It blinded him to their faults in many ways. Particularly with Trey. All he wanted was for the family to get along and for everyone to be happy."

"Do you believe your husband may have resented the extra financial support he gave to his brother?" he queried.

She shook her head. "No. He was proud of Bill. He would have done anything for him."

"I presume as a member of the family, Del was more than adequately compensated," Ethan mused.

Kayla gave a sharp laugh. "Oh, yeah. Next to Tyrone and Bill, Trey and Del had interests in the firm exponentially larger than the most senior associates. Even Harold. Of course, they couched Bill's income as profit sharing, like they do for Judge Walton."

"It makes sense, considering Trey and Del were actively working at the firm," Michelle conceded.

Kayla shook her head. "I'm willing to believe they were stealing pensioners' Social Security checks, and defrauding Uncle Sam, but I can't see any of them taking it so far as to have Ty and Trey murdered."

"Maybe you're suffering the same sort of blindness your husband exhibited," Ryan suggested quietly.

She turned to look at him, but rather than anger, he saw hurt and betrayal in her bright blue gaze. "What do you mean?"

"You can't see any of them purposely wanting to harm Tyrone and Trey because they were your family, too. Because, like Ty, you believe the possibility of them inflicting harm on Ty and Trey to be unfathomable."

"You're saying you think Del pulled the trigger," she concluded, her voice breaking.

Ryan inclined his head slightly. "The only thing wealthy people like more than money is more money," he said quietly. "And the only thing they fear more than anything in the world is somebody taking their money away from them. Didn't you tell me Ty was laser-focused on maintaining the family's wealth?"

"I can't imagine—"

Ryan cut her off by raising one hand. "I know you can't. It should be unthinkable for you. For any person with a conscience. But would it be for them?"

"You think he did it," she said softly.

"We have to assume he did, Kayla." He held her gaze, ignoring the searing pain in his leg as he sat up straighter on the sofa, planting his good foot on the floor for leverage. "And we have to assume they will stop at nothing to clean up any loose ends."

"Loose ends like me," she repeated, her expression disconcertingly placid.

"Yes."

"I can't hide from them forever," she argued.

He shook his head at her stubbornness. "As far as I'm concerned, you can't risk them catching up to you. Remember, you said you'd do things my way. You promised you wouldn't fight me on this."

"But—"

"No buts. You agreed you wouldn't push back. I'm holding you to your promise now. We're leaving here, Kayla. Tonight." Turning to Michelle, he asked, "Were you able to set something up?"

She nodded once, then met Kayla's gaze with a wince. "I'm sorry, but I agree with Ryan on this one. You have to go. I've arranged for you to stay in an FBI safe house a few hours from here. I can't say where, but Ryan will get you there. We have to know you're safe so we can focus all our energies on flushing Powers out of the underbrush."

Ryan studied Kayla's profile, but she'd remained disconcertingly stoic throughout Michelle's recitation.

Every muscle in his body tensed as she rose gracefully from her chair. If he was going to have to go toe-to-toe with her, he wished he could actually do it on two feet.

"Kayla, it is for the best," Ethan interjected.

But Kayla remained true to her word. She didn't argue. She didn't push back. Instead, she turned to Michelle and asked, "How long should I pack for?"

Which left him feeling even more agitated than any argument she might have mustered.

Chapter Fifteen

True to her word, she didn't argue, or push back in any way. She sat quietly while Ryan, Ethan and Michelle mapped out next steps, seething inside as she toyed with the remote connected to the smart-home system.

All around her, plans swirled. They'd leave after nightfall. It was smarter to use the old Range Rover stored in the garage in case they needed to go off road. Del Powers knew their vehicles, so there's no way they could take her luxury car or Ryan's state-issued SUV, but hopefully he'd forgotten about the ancient four-wheel drive stored in the garage.

She had no clue what their destination would be. The only thing she knew for certain was they would drive north, over the border into Missouri. Michelle had arranged for them to stay a night at an FBI safe house, but they would have to move on the following morning. When her friend apologized to Kayla for the inevitable rounds of movement, both Ryan and Ethan insisted it was the best plan for the immediate future.

She couldn't go anywhere Del Powers would expect her to turn up. She couldn't risk being seen in any of the places where she might be recognized. Heaven only knew how many snitches Del and his father had stashed around the northwest corridor.

Like the good soldier she was, she'd gone upstairs and packed a weekender bag of casual, comfortable clothes and only the barest necessities in terms of cosmetics and toiletries. For the first time since she'd left law school, Kayla Powers was planning to travel with only two pairs of shoes—the trainers she wore, and a pair of hiking boots.

Exhausted by the thought of living out of a bag for the foreseeable future, she dropped heavily onto the edge of the bed. Pulling her phone from her pocket, she saw she had a missed call from an unknown number. Normally, she wouldn't have paid it any mind, but she saw the icon for a voice mail was lit. Curious, she pressed Play.

"It doesn't have to be like this."

Her heart thudded to a stop when she recognized Del Powers's voice. Sitting up straighter, she darted a glance at the open door before pressing the phone to her ear hard. Her instincts told her this call from Del might be the key to her freedom.

"We always worked well together, Kayla. You can't hide forever," he said, his tone disconcertingly calm. "We need to meet. You and me. No cops. We need to sort this out once and for all."

The call ended, but his final words sent a chill racing down her spine.

Once and for all.

Did he expect her to hand over everything Ty had

entrusted to her and walk away? Or maybe he didn't expect her to walk away at all.

Either way, Del's calm demeanor was what scared her most. How did he expect this to play out? There was no way this could end well. Would it ever end?

After dropping her phone, she propped her elbows on her knees and dipped her head into her hands.

"Are you all set? We need to get moving."

Ryan's question should have startled her, but she was beyond being scared at this point. She'd heard his heavy footfalls and uneven gait coming down the hall. Ryan was treating his injury as if it didn't matter. But it did. If Del did get to her, Ryan would throw himself between her and danger, and she wasn't sure she could stand it if he was hurt any worse than he already was.

"Almost." Leaving the zip half-open, she headed into her bathroom, needing one more minute to think without the weight of Ryan's watchful gaze on her.

She drew three deep breaths to steel herself, then grabbed a handful of hair bands and a tube of facial cleanser she didn't need. Given the promises she'd made, stealing moments to sort her thoughts was the only acceptable means of rebellion available to her.

She could claim she was being coerced.

An argument could be made he'd put her in an untenable position, coaxing a promise from her under duress, but it would do no good.

Catching sight of his face as she reemerged from the bathroom, Kayla registered the stubborn resignation hardening his jaw. Sergeant Hastings had dug in, and unless she was willing to engage in endless hours of tug-of-war, she needed to cooperate.

Or give the appearance of cooperating.

She tossed the random items she'd grabbed into her bag and zipped it shut. Looping the strap over her shoulder, she let it fall against her hip as she walked away from the big comfortable bed.

Kayla had no idea what sort of arrangements to expect at an FBI safe house, but she was certain 2000-thread-count sheets wouldn't be one of the amenities.

She drew to a halt in front of him, lifting a single eyebrow in challenge, but he didn't step aside to allow her to leave.

"How about you? Do you need help packing?"

Ryan snorted. "My bag is in the car."

"Ah, you came to hurry me along."

"You being cooperative makes me nervous," he admitted bluntly.

She tipped up her chin and met his gaze. "Me being cooperative feels unnatural," she said with an edge to her voice. "But a promise is a promise. I am not arguing, and I'm not pushing back."

Ryan tilted his head. "Thank you."

"You're welcome. Shall we?" She waved her hand to indicate he was standing in her way. But he didn't move.

"Thank you," he repeated. "I'm not trying to make you unhappy. I only want you to be safe."

Instinctively, she covered her stomach with her hand and drew a steadying breath. "I appreciate your efforts."

They stood staring at one another for the space of a few thrumming heartbeats, then Ryan seemed to snap out of a trance. "Okay," he said a shade too briskly. "Here—" he reached out to lift the strap from her shoulder "—let me take your bag."

Kayla swiveled so the bag swung out of his grasp. "I can carry it. You need to hang on to the banister as we go down the steps. If you topple, I can't catch you."

No sooner were the words out of her mouth, Kayla regretted them. She didn't want to infer his injury made him incapable of doing whatever he needed to do to protect her. She had all the faith in the world in his dedication to her safety. The only issue was, she was not on board for the plan to cut and run that the rest of them had concocted.

"I'm not going to fall down the stairs," he said mulishly.

She gave a sympathetic chuckle. "Don't take this as an indictment of my faith in you, but I'm sure you won't mind if I walk behind you. I don't want to risk being crushed in the avalanche."

"Ha. Ha," Ryan said dryly over his shoulder as he made his way to the staircase.

Stiffness in each of his steps made her wince. As they painstakingly made their way down the steps, she couldn't help replaying the scene at the gatehouse in her head.

The stomach-roiling stench.

His hand warm on the center of her back.

The shadowy movement in the trees.

Del.

Now she had absolutely no doubt whatsoever she had seen somebody in a small boat that morning. If given a stack of bibles to swear on, she would affirm to the entire world she had spotted Delray Powers watching her from the woods as she heaved up her guts.

As they rounded the landing and started down the final flight of steps, she kept her gaze squarely centered on Ryan's broad shoulders. She'd watched him run toward danger, willingly placing himself between her and whatever lurked in the woods surrounding the house.

He hadn't hesitated. He hadn't locked up. He'd taken off in pursuit of the person he believed to be a threat to her and her unborn child.

As long as she lived, she would never forget the sight of Ryan running headlong into the trees. She'd never get over those endless minutes she'd waited, panting for breath, doing her best to escape the stench of Del's unsubtle message, but staying within range of the spot where Ryan had disappeared.

When she'd finally found a precious pocket of fresh air around the curve in the driveway, her worries had shifted from battling back another round of dry heaves to the notion she may have seen Ryan for the last time. She'd stood frozen, her hands braced on her knees and her eyes fixed on the tree line, listening for gunshots or calls for help.

She'd heard none of the above.

But when Ryan emerged from the trees, she could see right away something was wrong. He must have literally been running on adrenaline because his limp had not been as pronounced as it was now. Whatever happened in the woods, it had done some serious damage.

"Stop watching me like I'm about to tumble over," he grumbled without looking back at her.

"What makes you think I'm looking at you at all? Sheesh, the ego on some people," she teased.

"Your eyes are like laser beams. I can feel the heat," he growled. He drew up at the foot of the stairs, his hand clutching the newel post as he waited for her to join him on the main level. "Stop worrying about me," he ordered.

"Stop telling me what to do," she retorted.

"I'm afraid I'm going to be doing a lot of telling you what to do for the foreseeable future, so you might as well get used to it," he said, quirking an eyebrow. "No arguing. No pushback."

"Have I argued? Have I pushed?" she asked, being sure to keep her tone maddeningly patient and calm

"No, and your cooperation is making me nervous."

"So you keep telling me." She gave him a sweet smile. "I like keeping you on your toes."

"I feel like a ballerina." He nodded in the direction of the garage. "Michelle is sending us a GPS pin in about thirty minutes. She asked you to text her once we're in Missouri."

Kayla rolled her eyes. "I can't help wondering if Del is getting a charge out of being treated like such a big threat."

He leveled a gaze on her. "He is a big threat. And the sooner you let go of your old notions of who Del Powers is or was, the safer and better off we'll all be."

Kayla raised both hands in surrender. "Okay, fine, you're right." She closed her fingers then flicked them open again as if chasing the notion away. "Del Powers is a stone-cold killer, and he's out to get me."

She'd intended the words as a joke. A little bit of dark humor to offset the seriousness of the scene, but the moment she'd spoken the words, she realized they rang true. At least on some level.

Drawing a deep breath, she squared her shoulders and gestured for Ryan to lead the way to the garage.

He picked up the security-system remote and issued instructions.

"Arm alarm system in five minutes," he ordered.

"Alarm system will be armed in five minutes," the computer-generated voice confirmed.

"Begin random security lighting sequence at twenty-two hundred hours," he instructed.

"Random security lighting sequence will commence at twenty-two hundred hours," the voice replied.

Satisfied, Ryan placed the remote on the edge of the kitchen counter and led the way into the breezeway to the detached garage.

The hatch on the Range Rover was open, awaiting her luggage. Kayla tossed her bag in beside his duffel and shut the rear door.

She made her way to the right side of the vehicle. It wasn't until Ryan had flung himself bodily into the front left seat that he realized she'd tricked him.

The vehicle was an import, and the steering wheel was on the right.

"What the—"

She cut off his protest by holding out her hand for the keys. "Ty had this shipped over years ago," she said, wiggling her fingers in a gimme motion. "Before they even started selling them here in the States."

"I can drive," he countered.

"I know you can," she said with the patience of a kindergarten teacher, "but it's a manual transmission. You won't be able to handle the clutch for long."

Kayla wasn't above enjoying the look of horror on his face as he took in the vehicle's stick shift and lack of modern communication devices. "I'm guessing there's no Bluetooth," he said as he slid into the passenger seat.

"Nope." She cranked the engine, pressed the button to raise the garage door, then put the car in Reverse, slinging an arm over the back of his seat. She craned her neck to look out the rear window. "No time to fuss about it now, though. We can't get trapped in here by our own security system," she reminded him.

Ryan grunted when she hit bumps in the rutted gravel drive at a speed slightly faster than she would normally undertake. The sensor on the gate picked up their approach, and the rusted iron swung inward. The second she could clear it, Kayla floored the accelerator and turned onto the secondary road, tires spinning on the loose rocks at the shoulder of the road.

Ryan glanced over at her as she ran the Rover through its gears, a wry smile tucked into the corner of his mouth. "Feel better?"

Kayla glanced up at the rearview mirror in time to see the gate swing shut. "Marginally."

Taking her foot off the gas, she allowed the car to shift down to a more reasonable speed. Once she heard the clunk of the gate latching, she took off toward the highway.

They rode in silence. Shifting smoothly through the progression of gears, she allowed her thoughts to swirl until they coalesced.

She turned onto the highway and pointed the SUV north, toward the state line.

"We're going to have to get some gas," she announced, checking the gauges. "We don't use this car often, so we have a little less than a quarter of a tank."

"What kind of mileage does it get?" he asked gruffly.

She shrugged. "Heck if I know." She glanced over at him and offered a small conciliatory smile. "I'm sure we've got enough to get to the next gas station. There's always one just inside over the state line. Most of these counties were dry up until a few years ago."

He nodded. "Selling beer, cigarettes and lottery tickets to Arkansans desperate for vice has always been a big moneymaker for the state of Missouri."

Sure enough, less than a quarter mile beyond the state line they were greeted by a brightly lit gas station advertising specials on 30-packs of beer and crowing about their low, low cigarette prices.

She pulled in at the pump, then chuckled at herself as she realized the tank was on the opposite side of the car. "Oops. Hang on a second."

When she had the vehicle properly aligned, she killed the engine and reached into her purse to extract her wallet. But when she pulled out a card, he waved it away.

"No cards. We can't risk being monitored. Need to use cash to pay for things as much as we can. Fake names and dummy accounts haven't worked for us so far," he said grimly.

Kayla clasped her wallet for a moment, debating. She'd extracted a wad of cash from the safe in Tyrone's office, she didn't volunteer to pay for the gas. She could see her chance to put her plan into action shimmering like a mirage in the distance.

Luckily, Ryan was already rolling out of the car. "You stay in the car. I'll pay, then we can pump,"

"Okay." She watched as he made slow, steady progress across the deserted apron and disappeared into the store.

The moment he was out of sight, a large pickup truck jacked up on mud tires and loaded with roof-mounted lights pulled in at the pump on the other side of the island. Two young men jumped down from the elevated cab. Knowing she'd never have a better opportunity, Kayla cranked the engine and pulled away from the pump.

Hooking a left onto the highway, she headed back in the direction from which they'd come. She prayed she had enough gas in the tank to carry out the plan she'd hatched while Ryan, Ethan and Michelle had discussed what to do with her.

When he emerged from the gas station mere minutes later, Ryan Hastings swore under his breath. He hustled back to the pump, but he wasn't imagining things. Kayla was gone.

She'd left him stranded.

And judging by the taillights glowing in the distance, she was heading back to Arkansas. He swore again, this time louder.

"Oh, dude," a young man in sagging jeans and a stretched-out Cardinals T-shirt crooned. "Was that your ride?"

"What?" He shook his head to clear it then turned to look at two twentysomethings staring at him with their mouths agape.

"Did your girlfriend take off and leave you here?" one asked.

"She's not my girlfriend," he said, latching on to one irrefutable fact.

"Well, not anymore, I'd say," he said with a laugh.

"Was it your car or hers? Cool how it's got the steering wheel on the wrong side and all," the second guy chimed in.

"Did you guys get in a fight or something?" the first guy asked, glancing over to where Kayla's taillights were disappearing over a rise in the road.

"Must have been one heck of a fight," the other said with a sympathetic grimace.

"No fight," Ryan replied numbly. "No pushback," he added, almost as an afterthought. He hadn't been wrong. Kayla's capitulation had come far too easily. "Damn," he said under his breath.

"You're better off, man. I mean, she was hot and all, but leaving a guy high and dry out here," the shorter guy said. "Totally cold."

"Do you live far? Do you need a lift somewhere?" the first guy asked, removing the pump handle from his gas tank.

"What?" Ryan asked. Then he shook his head hard. "No. I mean, yes," he said, unable to get his thoughts and words in the right order. Coming to his senses, he fumbled for his wallet and flipped out his badge and ID. "Arkansas State Police, Sergeant Ryan Hastings. I need your vehicle."

The taller guy edged closer to the driver-side door. Ryan could literally pick him up and physically set the scrawny kid aside if he had to, but he was looking for their cooperation.

The kid reached for the door handle and hauled himself up into the cab of the truck again. "Dude, I understand you're having lady trouble, but I'm not giving you my truck."

"I'm not asking," Ryan said more forcefully, stepping into the open doorway and blocking the kid's ability to shut him out. "This is official business. I need to borrow your vehicle."

"Don't give it to him, Danny," his friend exhorted, scuttling back to the passenger side. "He's Arkansas State Police—this is Missouri, he doesn't have jurisdiction here," his buddy said as he hoisted himself into the vehicle.

"Please," Ryan said in a clipped tone. "I'm asking for your assistance. The woman you saw is being stalked. I need to go after her. She's about to put herself in grave danger."

"Grave danger," the kid named Danny repeated in a tone half awed and half terrified. "How do you mean?"

"There's somebody after her," Ryan explained in a rush. He placed a foot on the running board and grabbed the handle inside the open door.

"How do we know you're not the stalker?"

"The woman you saw is being harassed by a guy

who's already killed two people. I've been tasked with protecting her," he said looking the driver directly in the eyes. "I'm asking for your help."

Danny eyed him skeptically for a moment, but then his curiosity won out. "Okay, man, you can get in, but I'm driving."

"I can't lead you into what might possibly be an ambush," Ryan insisted.

"Our way or the highway, Mr. Arkansas State Policeman," his friend said in a singsong voice.

"This isn't a joyride. I'm serious about the danger," Ryan insisted, holding eye contact with Danny and ignoring his annoying buddy.

Without breaking the stare, Danny leaned forward and pulled the lever to move his seat forward. "Then you'd better climb in. She's getting a good head start on you."

Ryan gulped down the urge to shout at this stubborn guy. Despite the pain in his leg, and the fury roiling in his gut, he launched himself into the truck's sad excuse for a rear bench seat. "Head south as fast as you can. I'll tell you where to turn off."

Danny revved the engine and powered up the array of after-market lighting. With a whoop and a holler from the guy riding shotgun, they took off after Kayla with a squeal of oversized tires.

Chapter Sixteen

She was five miles into Arkansas before he called the first time.

"What the hell do you think you're doing," Ryan demanded.

Kayla chose to believe he was shouting to be heard over the roar of a barely muffled engine, and not yelling at her. "I'm heading back."

"I figured," he said in a disgruntled shout. "The question is why? You said you'd go along with the plan."

"I said I wouldn't fight you. I said I wouldn't give you any pushback." He muttered something unflattering about lawyers, and she could swear she caught the rumble of masculine laughter.

"You're failing to make your case, counselor," he said in an ominous tone.

"Where are you? Who are you with?" she asked when she heard another man say something she couldn't quite make out.

"This is your idea of not fighting me?"

Kayla bit her lower lip. She heard the hurt and worry he tried to cover up with grumbles and complaints. "I didn't fight you. I simply came up with an alternate plan," she said, her tone patronizing in its patience.

"You cannot go back to the lake house, Kayla," he said sternly.

"I am going back. What's more, I'm inviting Del over for a visit—"

"How? He hasn't been big on returning phone calls and texts lately."

"No one is calling the right number," she informed him.

Her assertion seemed to knock him off balance. For a moment, all she could hear was the rumble of an engine running at full throttle.

"He's been in contact with you," he concluded, not bothering to mask the disgust and betrayal in his tone.

"I had a voice mail today," she informed him. "It *was* Del we saw in the woods. He must be using a burner phone because the call came from an unknown number."

"Forward it to me," he ordered.

Kayla pulled the phone away from her ear as she glanced nervously at the winding mountain road ahead of her. "I can't right now. I'm driving."

"Kayla," he growled in a warning tone.

"I don't have hands free," she reminded him.

"Use the voice command," he insisted.

"I will, but first, I need you to call in the cavalry. I'm going to lure him to the house, but I need people ready to spring the trap."

"Kayla, you are not—"

"I'm the only one he'll come for, Ryan," she interrupted. "I'm the one who is in his way."

"You can't…the baby," he responded, but his words were broken into pieces.

She was entering one of the deep valleys where cell reception grew choppy. Knowing she needed to get her call in to Del as she came over the next rise, she spoke over his objections.

"I have to go now. Call Ethan, Michelle, whoever you want, but tell them to wait until I give the signal. I don't mind being bait, but I refuse to be chum," she warned him.

"Kayla, wait—"

"Ryan, believe me when I tell you I know I have a lot to live for, but I want to be able to live. Really live. You must trust me."

She paused, hoping he'd give her his blessing, if only grudgingly, before she ended the call, but he said nothing.

"I'll send you the contact information. Goodbye, Ryan. And thank you," she added, almost as an afterthought. "I do appreciate what you tried to do for me."

She dropped the phone into her lap, her fingertip hovering over the icon that would end the call. She didn't want their connection to end, but if she wanted a shot at being able to crawl out from under the specter of Del Powers, she needed to draw him out of the shadows.

"Kayla, I—"

Whatever Ryan was about to say was lost when she hit a bump in the road and her finger grazed the touch-sensitive screen, ending the call.

The drone of worn tires on ancient asphalt hummed loud in her ears. She wet her lips as she glanced down at the now-darkened screen. "Yeah. I know. Me, too," she whispered into the darkness around her.

She drove the rest of the way back to the house as fast as she dared on the dark country roads. The moment she turned off the highway, onto the private road leading to the lake house, she rolled her shoulders back and gripped the steering wheel with both hands. Calling out to her phone's virtual assistant, she issued a command. "Replay last message in my voice-mail box on speaker."

The moment Del's voice pierced the safety of her vehicle, she cut it off by ordering the assistant to return the call to the stored phone number.

Del did not answer. She didn't expect him to. Instead, she continued to play the game, offering herself up as the mouse to his cat.

"It's me. I've ditched Sergeant Hastings, and I'm back at the house on the lake. This is your one and only chance, Delray," she said, drawling his full name as she waited for the gate to creak open. "You think I took what's rightfully yours? Well, come and get me. If you have the guts."

Then she shot up the driveway, leaving the gate wide open.

She parked the Range Rover in its usual spot, strode through the breezeway and entered the house the same way they'd left it. Grabbing the security remote, she ordered, "Disarm system. Standby mode."

"System disarmed," came the reply.

Her mind reeling with all there was to do, she made a mental list.

Light. She needed to light every corner of the house

up. She wanted no dark corners where Del could slip into the shadows.

"Lights on, all rooms."

Every bulb in the house sprang to life. *"Lights on,"* the virtual assistant confirmed.

Moving through the kitchen, Kayla made her way over to the glass sliders. The patio, dock and boathouse were floodlit. Catching her bottom lip between her teeth, she manually flipped the switches to shut off the exterior lights.

Satisfied, she hurried down the hall to Ty's office. There, she locked herself in and moved to the safe. She removed the gun her husband kept there. Her father was a hunter, so respect for firearms had been drilled into her from an early age. Ty had taken her with him to the shooting range a few times, insisting it was important she knew how to load and use the handguns he kept in both houses.

Kayla opened the safe and withdrew the gun and the clip of bullets. She wasn't particularly fond of the notion of carrying a loaded weapon around, but she wasn't about to face down Del Powers unarmed.

If her plan worked, she wouldn't actually have to face him at all.

With the gun loaded, but the safety on, she reached into the safe one more time, this time withdrawing a key attached to a neon yellow foam floater. The boat key hadn't been removed from the safe since the state police had released Trey's precious ski boat. It was the only time she'd ever known her husband to take something away from his spoiled heir.

The key dangled by a beaded chain as she lifted the

security remote and pressed the button. "Intercom on," she ordered as she headed for the sliding doors.

"Communications system activated."

To test it, she lifted the remote again and said, "Can you hear me now?"

The echo of her own voice bounced back at her from the depths of the cavernous house.

"Record all video and audio," she ordered.

"Recording in progress," the system confirmed.

A grim smile curved her lips. She moved to Tyrone's computer and woke the system. The oversized monitor displayed a grid of all camera angles. One by one, she cycled through them, inspecting each frame for anything out of the ordinary. Only those arrayed along the back of the house were dark and grainy, but the ambient lighting from the house lit them enough for her to make out shapes and movement.

Everything was quiet. For the moment.

She held her phone poised, ready to call Ryan the moment she spotted any sign of Del's truck. But no one came.

Or so she thought.

It seemed like hours had passed before the front door opened and closed, but it was likely only minutes.

"Kayla?" Del Powers called up to the cathedral ceiling of the entry.

Panicking, she dialed Ryan's number. This wasn't what she planned. She thought she'd see him come up the drive and slip out the back. Now she was stuck. Ryan answered on the first ring.

"What the hell are you doing?" he snapped. "Answer my calls."

"Shh." She turned down the volume on her phone as low as it would go. "Del is in the house."

Ryan let loose with an expletive, and whoever was with him immediately asked what was wrong.

She moved over to the office door and pressed her thumb to the biometric pad that would engage the locks. "I'm in the safe room. I'm armed. I have a plan, but I need you to calm down and listen."

"Oh, dude, you're in deep now," one of the guys in the background said on a guffaw.

"Shut it, Jimmy," another man snapped. "I think this is serious stuff, man."

"Who are you with?" she asked. But before she could answer, Del called out for her again. "Never mind. Mute your phone. I'm going to leave the call open. You have backup coming?"

"Yes," Ryan replied tightly. "Kayla—"

"Mute it. I can't have you giving me away."

Almost immediately, all the noise on the other end went silent.

She eyeballed the video capture of her late husband's nephew. His hair was longer and messier than she'd ever seen. He wore tree-patterned hunting camouflage from head to toe and sturdy boots. This version of Del Powers looked nothing like the tax attorney she'd known for years. This Del Powers had tried to shoot her, stalked her and wanted to take everything Tyrone had treasured from her. Maybe even her baby.

She lifted the smart remote with a trembling hand. "I'm upstairs," she said over the intercom. "I, uh, I spilled some wine, so I needed to change clothes."

On camera, she saw Del sneer as he turned his face

toward the staircase. "I guess the trip to rehab didn't take, huh?"

His sarcastic tone set her teeth on edge, but she did her best to keep a rein on her temper. "Hard to focus on staying healthy when someone is trying to kill you." Drawing a shaky breath, she continued. "We always got along, Del. I don't get it. What did I ever do to you?"

He gave a short bark of laughter, then strode to the steps. "You married into the wrong family."

Kayla held her breath as she watched him slowly creep up the first few stairs. "Come on," she whispered under her breath encouragingly. "Come and get me."

Del climbed another two steps. "It was supposed to be you, you know," he said with such equanimity her blood ran cold.

Glancing down at her phone, she saw the call to Ryan was still in progress, but she didn't dare try to take on multiple conversations. Not when she was watching a man who wanted to kill her creep up her stairs.

She tapped out a quick text. You getting all this?

His reply came in an instant. 10-4

Focusing on the footage of Del, she lifted the remote. "Supposed to be me what?" she asked, dreading the answer she was fairly sure she already knew.

"You cuddled up on the couch with good old Uncle Ty," he said, his voice growing louder with remembered anger. "I don't know why I thought that hillbilly Harley Jenkins could do the job right."

"Harley Jenkins? What job?" she asked, needing more information.

"You and Uncle Ty."

Kayla stared at the monitor incredulously. Had he

shrugged and told her he planned to execute her? Genuinely bewildered, she spoke into the remote. "You hired Harley Jenkins to kill Tyrone and me?"

Del snorted, then started taking the stairs two at a time. "He took my money, but said he couldn't go through with it. You know what they say about wanting a job done right."

The moment she saw him reach the upper gallery, she moved away from the computer and to the door. "You did kill them."

"If it's any consolation, it was quick," he said in a mocking tone. "They never saw me as any threat."

Needing to draw him out, she asked the burning question. "Why? How could you?"

"Why? Why should you have everything I had coming to me?" he demanded, his voice rising again.

"What do you mean? You didn't know Ty changed his will."

"Oh, but I did. My jerk of a cousin made sure I knew."

"Trey knew? How?"

"He found a copy of the will in Daddy's office. You thought you were so smart, having someone else draw it up, but you underestimated how much of a mama's boy old Trey was. He didn't like you taking his mommy's spot on the gravy train."

Shaking her head, she spoke into the microphone. "I didn't—"

Above her, she heard a door slam against a wall. "Where the hell are you?" he shouted.

Knowing she had to get out while he was occupied, she pressed her thumb to the scanner. It was risky to leave the safe room, but if Del realized there was no way he could get to her, he would flee the scene. She would lose her chance to be free of him.

But nothing happened.

She juggled her phone, the key chain and the remote, shifting them all into her left hand. Squaring up in front of the scanner, she pressed her right thumb to the screen again, whispering a prayer under her breath.

Her shoulders sagged as the locks disengaged.

"Kayla!"

She knew she had to come up with something quick. "Oh, I'm in the blue suite," she said, trying to control her breathing. "Couldn't stay in the master after…" She let the thought trail off as she made her way down the hall, her sights set on the back of the house.

His heavy footsteps seemed to echo through the house. "Why not? It's all yours now," he replied.

Inside the service door of the kitchen, she stopped to taunt him one last time in hopes of getting a full confession. She lifted the remote again. "It wouldn't have been, though. If you killed Ty and me, you'd still have to deal with Trey."

"Turns out, he was easier to deal with than you," he growled. "Stop wasting my time."

"You know you aren't going to get away with this. You know the police are looking for you."

"They can look all they want. I can make it so they never find me."

She opened the door but drew up short at his answer. "Then, why? You know it will never be yours now. Why go through all this?"

"Because it should have been," he growled between

gritted teeth. "It should have been mine all along. My father should have made sure everything came to me, but as usual, Daddy was too busy being a big shot. Well, he won't be for long, will he?"

Kayla's eyes widened as she realized Del had planned to take them all down one by one. She wanted a moment to process it all, but she didn't dare hang around one second longer. Time was not on her side. There would be no reasoning with him. Del had nothing left to lose.

With the house lit up brighter than an octogenarian's birthday cake, she moved away from the windows as quickly as possible. Heading alongside the darkened patio, she hurried toward the boathouse. Once she felt the darkness close in around her, she shoved the security remote into her pocket and raised the phone to her ear.

"How far are you?" she asked, breathless.

"Close to the drive. County guys are behind us. Ethan and Michelle twenty minutes out."

"Were you able to hear—"

"I heard it all," he assured her. "Get out of the house."

"I'm out. I'm recording, and I can talk to him, but I won't be able to hear him anymore."

"Get as far away from him as you can. It's dark, so head for the woods."

Kayla shook her head and headed for the dock. "I have a better idea. Listen, something tells me he'll keep talking, but we both know whatever we get may not be admissible in court. Del will know it, too," she informed him, her sneakers slapping against the aluminum planking of the boat dock.

"Where are you?"

"Getting out of here," she panted as she reached for

the strap attached to the canvas cover of Trey's flashy red ski boat and yanked it free with one hand. The boat was in its slip, covered tight as a drum and untouched by anyone in the Powers family since the night Mallory Murray had gone overboard.

Moving frantically, she unlatched two straps along the side, then realized she couldn't peel back enough of the cover to get to the driver's seat. "Hang on," she huffed into the phone, then shoved it into the front of her shirt so she could use both hands. Moving to the other side, she quickly released three straps, yanked the cover back far enough to open the cockpit and stepped over the gunnel into one of the pristine white seats.

Taking her spot behind the wheel, she closed her eyes and prayed the engine would turn over.

Kayla winced when the powerful boat roared to life, but she couldn't worry about the noise now—she had seconds to get this boat free of its slip and out of range of whatever weaponry Del may have brought. She let the engine idle at a purr as she unwrapped ropes from the cleats and gave as powerful a shove as she could. The boat drifted back, the bumpers tied to each side knocking against the aluminum dock. She didn't have the time or inclination to worry about being careful.

Easing the throttle up, she reversed until she was well clear of the other boats. Then and only then, did she allow herself to glance at the house. Flashes of blue lights streaked the trees. The police were arriving.

Del's tall, lumbering figure appeared at the sliding doors to the patio. She cranked the wheel and brought the nimble boat around as a shout of frustrated rage echoed across the still waters of the inlet.

She didn't turn on the running lights. She knew the sound of the engine was a giveaway, but in the darkness it would be difficult for him to pinpoint her exact location once she got far enough from the shore. Something skipped and plunked into the water to her left, but it was too dark and she was too panicked to see what it was. A fish? A bullet?

Pointing the nose of the boat toward the widest part of the lake, she pushed the throttle forward and prayed she could make it past the spit of land that marked the entrance to the cove. Once she was beyond the curve, she could risk a light. Hopefully, once she was around the corner, maybe the police would have Del in custody.

This time, she heard the crack of a rifle being fired, but she had no idea where the bullet went. As long as it wasn't into her or this boat, she didn't care. Let him keep firing at her. Keeping his focus locked on her would allow Ryan and his backup to get the drop on him.

Hair whipping around her face, she sped into the darkness, and shouted into the wind, "You can't take my life. I won't let you."

Then, as she cut the wheel to arc wide left to follow the jagged shoreline, she pulled back on the throttle and glanced back at the house before it disappeared from view. Blinking in disbelief, she gave her head a shake.

"What the—"

She could have sworn she'd seen a jacked-up pickup complete with a half-dozen rooftop lights parked on the lake-house patio.

She steered the boat closer and spotted Special Agent Ryan Hastings kneeling beside a person stretched face-down on the ground, his head turned toward the water. Cranking the wheel, she pushed forward on the throttle. A plume of water rooster-tailed behind the boat as she came around.

She fumbled for her phone, the remote for the security system tumbling out of her pocket as she yanked it free. "Are you there?" she panted into the phone.

But Ryan didn't respond. She watched as two officers rushed over to take the person she assumed was Del into custody. She tossed the phone onto the seat as Ryan pushed to his feet. She kept her gaze locked on him as he stumbled.

Was he hurt?

She sped up. As she approached, she spotted his gun dangling at his side as he raised his free hand as if to shield his eyes. She saw him scanning the water beyond the glow of the light spilling from the house.

He was looking for her.

Her hammering heart slowed to a steady *thud-thud-thud*. She flipped on the boat's running lights and gave a short blast of the horn.

A flood of calm washed through her the moment he spotted her. She killed the engine, allowing momentum to carry her toward the shore.

"Are you okay?" she shouted. But he clearly couldn't hear her. Remembering the remote, she scooped it from the deck of the boat and pressed the button. "Are you okay?"

Ryan glanced back at the house, then turned back to the water. She could see the smirk twisting his lips. He shouted something back, but though the sound carried, the words were too garbled for her to hear.

She shook her head. Then, she saw the deputies behind him helping a handcuffed man to his feet.

Del.

They had Del. It was done.

"We got him," she whispered to herself.

She saw Ryan reaching for his back pocket as two gangly guys in T-shirts and baggy jeans started down the dock, gesticulating to the action on the patio. When he raised his phone to his ear, she grabbed hers again.

"Are you okay?" she said breathlessly.

"I'm fine," he answered gruffly. "You?"

"I'm…" She paused, breathless. "We got him."

"We got him," he confirmed.

In no hurry to be lectured on her scheme, she continued to let the boat drifted closer to the dock rather than piloting it to its slip.

"Dude, that was so cool," one of the guys approaching him crowed.

"You totally took that guy down," the other chimed in.

"Ryan?" She couldn't contain the smile spreading across her face as she recognized the tricked-out pickup from the gas station. "Did you make some new friends?"

Chapter Seventeen

Ryan didn't answer her impertinent question.

She tried to hide her smile when he made an impatient gesture for her to bring the boat in, but she could see the relief written all over his face. She'd scared him almost as much as she'd scared herself. But she did what she had to do to stop this madness, and no matter how fiercely Ryan Hastings scowled, she would do it again.

Del had confessed to killing Tyrone and Trey.

He was in custody.

She was free.

Letting the boat drift, she lifted her gaze to the pseudo castle the first Tyrone Delray Powers had built as a testament to his wealth and power. The place where she'd fallen in love with his son. The house that became her refuge when she was miserable, and eventually, the key to her freedom.

A gentle wave of sadness washed through her as she realized she could never live there.

The happy memories she had there, the solace she'd once found within its walls, would forever be tainted now. Shadows of Trey's negligence, the emptiness left behind by Ty's murder and this terrifying night would lurk in every corner. But she would retain control of the firm. Or what was left of it, if the fallout from multiple scandals didn't bring the place down entirely.

Her thoughts were interrupted by Ryan shouting her name.

She glanced up to find him standing firm at the end of the dock, his hands cupped around his mouth. Giving her head a shake, she raised a hand in acknowledgment, then pointed to the boathouse and slips, her eyebrows raised in question.

He shook his head and pointed an emphatic finger at the swim dock where he was standing. His visible relief had transformed into a thunderous expression. Behind him, the two young men she assumed belonged with the pickup truck jostled and crowed about the scene around them.

Biting her bottom lip to keep from smiling, she gave the boat enough juice for her to turn the starboard side perpendicular to the end of the dock. Cutting the engine, she allowed the wake to carry the craft closer as she yanked back more of the half-loosened cover to look for a line she could toss to him.

The bumpers she never bothered to pull into the boat nudged the dock. She heard a groan of pain and looked up to see Ryan struggling to lower himself enough to grab one of the bumpers and haul the boat closer.

"Don't! Your knee," she cried, finally coming up with one of the nylon ropes used to tow inflatable tubes. She loosened one end, then tossed the gathered line to Ryan. "Hold on to this."

He straightened, not bothering to mask the twist of pain that contorted his handsome face. "Get up here."

"I'm trying," she said as she secured her end. Then, diving under the canvas, she extracted another rope and went about unfurling it. "This would have been easier at the boathouse," she grumbled, scooting around to find a spot to attach the second rope.

"Hey, we can help," one of Ryan's companions said, boots clomping as he hurried to help Ryan's side. "That was awesome."

"It wasn't awesome, Danny," Ryan growled, shoving the rope at the taller guy. "It was foolish. Reckless. Deadly."

Kayla smirked as she nodded to the shorter of the two, who stood poised to catch her rope. "He's right. Don't try this at home."

With the boat tethered to the end of the dock, Kayla climbed onto the seat, then stepped onto the side of the boat, holding her arms out to maintain her balance.

"Give me your hands," Ryan ordered.

"No," she said briskly. She waved at the man he'd called Danny. "You help me. He's hurt."

Danny and his companion hurried to the edge to do her bidding, but not without cracks about how the old man should step aside, in addition to offers to fetch Ryan a walker. The second her feet hit the dock, she thanked them politely for their help, then turned to face the music.

Ryan stared at her, his expression cycling from fury to relief, from admiration to agony. She was certain there were a half-dozen others to come, but the pain etched into the brackets around his mouth tugged on something elemental inside her.

She wanted to kiss him and make it all better.

Grasping his beautiful face in both hands, she stepped into him, her thumbs smoothing the lines of pain. She searched his eyes for signs of resistance as she stretched up to meet him. She saw none, so she gave in to instinct and pressed her mouth to his.

Ryan's arms closed around her, clasping her to him tightly. A tremor ran through them both. She shifted her hands into his thick, soft hair and held him there, angling her head in an invitation to deepen the kiss.

Behind them, the guys who'd helped Ryan whooped and hollered. Kayla found she couldn't stop smiling when he shifted to take the kiss deeper. Ryan's lips curved against hers in response, and he pulled back and pressed his forehead to hers.

"Well, this is an interesting turn of events," said a familiar voice.

Kayla was too drawn into Ryan's intense gaze for her brain to process it. He was panting softly. Each puff of breath whispered across her damp lips made her ache to pull him back into the kiss.

"Ethan, don't," Michelle said in a harsh whisper. "Leave them alone."

"I've wanted to kiss you since the day I met you," he said, ignoring the commentary.

"Liar," she whispered in a shaking voice. "You thought I was a pain in the backside."

"Still wanted to kiss you."

"When you two get a minute," Ethan called to them.

"Hush," Michelle snapped.

Kayla drew a deep breath, resigning herself to the interruption. Looking deep into Ryan's eyes, she said, "We need to talk."

"Understatement," Ryan replied.

"But first we need to fill in Ethan on Del, then we need to get someone to look at your knee."

His hands came to rest on her waist, his thumbs grazing the curve of her belly. He maintained eye contact as he pulled up to his full height. "You should be checked out, too."

A sudden rush of doubt swamped her. She was pregnant. What was she thinking? No man was going to want to get involved with a woman who was carrying another man's baby.

Her thoughts must have shown on her face, because Ryan swooped in and pecked another gentle kiss to her lips. "We'll talk."

"Okay."

"I'm not done with you," he said, holding her tight and gazing deeply into her eyes. "Things will be complicated and confusing, and a giant mess, but I won't be your Frank Farmer."

"Huh?" She reared back, searching his eyes for some clue as to what he meant.

"I'm not going to let you kiss me then take off on your private jet. You get me?" he asked, bending to pin her with a penetrating stare.

"I don't have a private jet."

"Good." He nodded briskly, then glanced over his shoulder at the small crowd gathering at the end of the dock. "As long as we can keep our feet on the ground, I think we'll figure everything else out."

* * * * *

#2157 MAVERICK DETECTIVE DAD
Silver Creek Lawmen: Second Generation • by Delores Fossen
When Detective Noah Ryland and Everly Monroe's tragic pasts make them targets of a vigilante killer, they team up to protect her young daughter and stop the murders. But soon their investigation unleashes a series of vicious attacks...along with reigniting the old heat between them.

#2158 MURDER AT SUNSET ROCK
Lookout Mountain Mysteries • by Debra Webb
A ransacked house suggests that Olivia Ballard's grandfather's death was no mere accident. Deputy Detective Huck Monroe vows to help her uncover the truth. But as dark secrets surrounding Olivia's family are exposed, she'll have to trust the man who broke her heart to stay alive.

#2159 SHROUDED IN THE SMOKIES
A Tennessee Cold Case Story • by Lena Diaz
Former detective Adam Trent is stunned to learn his cold case victim is alive. But Skylar Montgomery is still very much in danger—and desperate for Adam's help. Their investigation leads them to one of Chattanooga's most powerful families...and a vicious web of mystery, intrigue and murder.

#2160 TEXAS BODYGUARD: WESTON
San Antonio Security • by Janie Crouch
Security Specialist Weston Patterson risks everything to keep his charges safe. But protecting wealthy Kayleigh Delacruz is his biggest challenge yet. She doesn't want a bodyguard. But as the kidnapping threat grows, she'll do anything—even trust Weston's expertise—to survive.

#2161 DIGGING DEEPER
by Amanda Stevens
When Thora Graham awakens inside a coffin-like box with no memory of how she got there, Deputy Police Chief Will Dresden, the man she left fifteen years ago, follows the clues to save her life. Their twisted reunion becomes a race against time to stop a serial killer's vengeful scheme.

#2162 K-9 HUNTER
by Cassie Miles
Piper Comstock and her dog, Izzy, live a solitary, peaceful life. Until her best friend is targeted by an assassin. US Marshal Gavin McQueen knows the truth—a witness in protection is compromised. It's dangerous to recruit a civilian to help with the investigation. But is the danger to Piper's life...or Gavin's heart?